Safe in the Date

Q. T. Porta

Grosvenor House
Publishing Limited

The right of Q. T. Porta to be identified as the author of this
work has been asserted in accordance with Section 78
of the Copyright, Designs and Patents Act 1988

The book cover is copyright to Q. T. Porta
Marie-Claire Ferreira handed the copyright to Q. T. Porta
Cover artwork by –
Marie-Claire Ferreira: Insta:@marieclairecreations.

This book is published by
Grosvenor House Publishing Ltd
Link House
140 The Broadway, Tolworth, Surrey, KT6 7HT.
www.grosvenorhousepublishing.co.uk

A CIP record for this book
is available from the British Library

ISBN 978-1-80381-905-1

Acknowledgements

It has taken a long time to complete a story showing how a crumbling community can be restored and strengthened.

In retrospect, my family have given support, surprises, and strife, however it would have been impossible to finish the novel without their empathy and encouragement.

The temptation is to only thank each person who offered kindness, but there is recognition for those who withdrew their word, because they inadvertently opened the door to new opportunities. They had a part to play but will not partake in the future chapters of my life.

The guidance and help from Grosvenor House Publishing Ltd is much appreciated and needed. I enjoyed writing essays in school and hoped for a gold star from the teacher. I retained that same level of hope for the next fifty years and with unrelentless joy can now say - "I am an author."

The artist Marie-Claire Ferreira created the front cover - capturing the meaning with sensitivity and brevity. Each intricate detail depicts a segment of the story. It has been a pleasure to have the opportunity to work with Marie-Claire: her artistry is sublime and is a true gift. She has been extremely patient after a few blips and trips in finishing the novel.

And last but by no means least, I thank you – the reader: for your generosity to buy the book, for your support and for each time you encourage others to share in the wonderment of reading.

In trust, the story will raise your spirits and shine a light towards the warm welcome that awaits you. The day and time may not fit in with your plans and you may not understand, but the author of creation has already completed the book.

Q. T. Porta
2024

CHAPTER 1

Ribbons of light shimmered up the aisle towards the arrangement of daffodils balancing beautifully in the new deep blue terracotta vase, specially purchased for the Easter Sunday service.

I felt a tug on my left arm which interrupted my meditation. Kiyana Jonas, the head of the junior choir, flustered and fraught with anxiety literally grabbed my attention. "Sorry to disturb you, I need your help, Jemima's hair is stuck and she's crying. Don't know what to do?"

I did not ask for further details during the prayers and waited until the congregation were enthusiastically singing the first verse of the hymn; '*Thine Be The Glory*' before making my way to the scene of the disquiet.

Jemima's curly hair was entangled in the office door handle and in the strings attached to the inflated yellow latex balloons. Tears streamed down Jemima's face, and she needed a handkerchief to blow her nose. My enquiry popped out too hurriedly, "how did this happen? No, sorry, not important now." I kneeled in front of Jemima, and then immediately worried how I could stand up again. The strength in my knee joints and muscles is fading fast due to a lack of exercise and too many years sitting at a desk. The sight of me rolling on the floor would not help in any shape or form.

"It's okay, we'll ask Mr Knotty to go away, and we'll be all okay."

The commotion attracted the attention of Ivee Chong, the Children & Families Minister, who looked perplexed at my impromptu nursery rhyme. "Mrs Abbott is going to be so angry. How can I explain this? How can I apologise?" The abundance of questions came from Ivee who had only been in the role since January. Concerns were raised with regards her age i.e., 23, especially from the more seasoned members of St Laurence - an Anglian Church in the village of Old Botlean in Hampshire. I placed my hand on her shoulder and whispered, "take a deep breath, we need to keep calm, for Jemima."

Mrs Abbott is the head of the local Women's Institute, an influential and forceful character in the community. I tried to persuade the Vicar not to use the large number of balloons, but he insisted on displaying a visible image of how we are celebrating '*He is Risen.*' The overall cost and overwhelming risk of asking the Junior Choir to hold the balloons as they walked towards the altar was too high for my liking, but the Church Wardens overruled by objection. Kiyana led the other members of the Youth Choir out to perform in front of a welcoming audience.

Ivee held Jemima's hand whilst I pulled gently on the string, but it was twisting tighter to the roots of her hair. "Ouch, it hurts, ow! I want my mum," Jemima cried.

"Mummy's sitting just outside and is looking forward to your solo." Ivee's attempt at comfort was not successful. I found the nail scissors in my rucksack and said, "don't worry Jemima, you'll be out with the choir in a few minutes. They are waiting for the star of the show." The snip into her curls lessened the grip and I cut the string to remove the last remnants caught in the handle." Jemima rushed out to harmonise with her friends. Cuttings of her curls rested on her shoulders. My mind raced to find a solution and thought, '*I cannot go out to brush them off.*'

"Well done, sweetheart. You were marvellous, give mummy a big hug." Mrs Abbot's proud announcement came to an abrupt halt once the appearance of the unscheduled haircut began to dawn on her. "What has happened to your hair!? Darling, are you okay? Who did this to you?" Mrs Abbot's raised voice drew a lot of attention. Jemima let go of the balloon in her right hand and pointed at me.

Mrs Abbot reacted angrily, "How dare you touch my daughter's hair. I am going to report you to the Vicar. That young woman; Ivee? She is the children's minister – where was she? Looking at her mobile as usual?!"

The Vicar intervened, "Mrs Abbot, I can see you are upset. Hannah will get you a cup of tea and we can sit down and have a conversation." Hannah, the vicar's wife, is petite, reserved in her style of clothes and wears minimal make up. Her highlighted bob hides the onset of grey hair, but wiry strands rise above the middle parting. She is a tremendous support to her husband and the community: her empathetic nature is a comfort for all the congregation especially when making regular home visits.

"Would you like a biscuit with your tea?" Hannah asked tentatively.

"NO! I want an explanation!" Mrs Abbot responded and flared her nostrils.

"Of course. I'll leave you in the capable hands of my husband. The volunteers need help in the kitchen."

"Mrs Abbott, I am sorry to see you so upset." The Vicar looked concerned and asked, "can you share what happened?"

"You should be explaining to me how you allow anyone to cut my daughter's hair. Ivee promised profusely Jemima would be safe. Should you be employing someone who is so inexperienced?"

Wilberforce Trent, the vicar, is tall and towers over members of the congregation. His slight frame accentuates his height, and his baldness makes him look older than his years, but he retains a youthful character. Although relatively new to the parish he drew on previous experience to respond to the accusations in a calm manner. "I apologise. You and Jemima are understandably upset. We take our safeguarding management seriously and our Officer will make a full report. Ivee is an asset to St Laurence and has made a great start. Clearly there has been an accident and we will find out all the details." Mrs Abbott's reddened face did not relax. "Well, clearly, Ivee needs to explain why she is neglecting her duties and to make it worse, your secretary is involved in this inappropriate behaviour to my daughter."

Wilberforce smiled gently and replied. "Ruth is an excellent P.A. Do not know how we would manage without her."

"Maybe you should start learning to manage without her." Mrs Abbott retorted. "You need professional staff who know how to act responsibly."

"Ruth is drafting a project plan for the long list of items and work required to update the church. We are thankful for her professional skills. I am sure there was no malicious intention and can only apologise once again for the distress." The vicar's explanation did not land well.

"Do not expect any more donations from me nor the W.I. until a full explanation in writing is presented. I must get back to Jemima. Poor darling, she was looking forward to being in the choir. I will have to take her to the hairdressers on Tuesday and will send you the bill." Mrs Abbott stormed off. I thought the heels of her shoes would break due to the force of each step hitting the floor.

Wilberforce looked up towards the yellow latex balloon affixed to the timber rafter beams and prayed for a peaceful resolution.

***

CHAPTER 2

I held on tightly to the small shaky step ladder underpinned with folded cards advertising the dates for the Community Lunch in May. The remnants of blue tac stubbornly stuck to the bunting and the lid of the maroon post box kindly donated by Lester Plumb, the manager of the village Post Office which I fear will have to close soon. The pace of change is uprooting the security of the community. Lester is small in stature but has broad shoulders and embraces the bachelor life. Rumours are rife around the parish after Lester was seen carrying a bouquet of flowers. The curtain twitchers are continuing with their enquiries. Much to their frustration there is no conclusive evidence.

Logic evades my mind at times of stress and the drive to complete the task overshadows the need to exercise prudence. My sensible trainers were safely sitting at the bottom of the wardrobe, so I wobbled in my blue court shoes. The beam of light coming through the window of the church hall, glided across the tables set out for the afternoon tea in celebration of St. George's Day.

"Please let me help," said Mervyn Hopkins.

I dared not deviate my line of sight fixed on a frayed piece of red ribbon clinging onto the grey flaking paint on the wall – a remnant from previous years. The concentration was preventing me from overbalancing. "Thank you," I replied in a high-pitched voice. "I need to go on a refresher course for my circus skills."

Mervyn Hopkins, weary from the weight of grief, wears a cloth cap in all weather and locations. His wife, Gwen, passed away last year shortly after their Ruby Wedding Anniversary. Attendance at services and events eases the sharpness of his pain but the emptiness in his eyes emanates the loneliness. "Gwen used to get all tangled up with the Christmas lights." Mervyn reminisced about the domestic bliss he shared with his childhood sweetheart. They moved from Swansea to Old Botlean to be close to Gwen's sister after Mervyn retired. Mervyn unravelled the flags twisted around the knotted ribbon. A conundrum requiring an experienced hand and an abundance of patience.

"Just warming up the tea pots and cups," said Molly. "Mammie would not use the tea pot until it had a bath in boiling hot water. Our old, knitted tea cosy was great. No good putting cold milk into cold tea, might as well have just a glass of milk. Save on the washing up. Do ye have the flowers? Empty vases won't be doing any good."

"Ivee's gone to get the daffodils from the church," I replied.

"They'll be a bit sorry for themselves by now. Wasn't the Vicar's wife goin' to the market? Be nice spring flowers there."

Molly's 1940's style wrap around apron is adorned with small daisies clustered on a green background. She takes her duties as a catering manager very seriously and is a dedicated volunteer. Logan, the caretaker, calls her a *busy body* which is harsh although a slither of truth runs through his judgement.

My response was hindered by the fear of falling off the ladder. I jittered, "Ivee said she will pick up the cakes when you're ready."

"She's not to worry," Molly replied, "Vicky was here at the crack of dawn; poor thing will fall down before she sits down. Himself needs to go into a care home. I've put the cakes in the tins with Santa on the lid. No one will know and am sure won't care as long as they have a full plate."

***

Victoria Beard owns 'Bake in the Past' – the village bakery with a shop front that would fit seamlessly into The Shambles - an historic street in York. I used to call her the "bread face woman" when in a particular cheeky mood. My come-uppance was a temporary ban on the sponge finger topped with vanilla icing: a Friday treat on the way home from school, to greet the weekend with gladness. The absence for two weeks felt like a lifetime, but my mum did not budge. She meant what she said and said what she meant. A firm but fair approach which still applies today even though I will be fifty in June.

My brother did not care much for cakes nor childish rebellion. He shares the gift of academia with dad. Both are studious but do not have an air of superiority. Gareth's skills and sturdiness brought him to live in Zürich. He excels in his profession as an Actuary and is married and has two children - Cedwyn and Ursula who thankfully have inherited their looks from their mother – Beatrice. They are truly comfortable in their own skins and enjoy living in a country where the outdoor lifestyle is encouraged and embraced from birth.

Molly busied herself re-arranging the red-rose cake stands and moving the red and white serviettes onto the side plates. Unfortunately, Ivee's tentative attempt at the place settings did not meet Molly's exacting standards. Molly shared the doubt of other members of the congregation about the decision to employ Ivee. The perception that her inaugural role means ineptitude will take time to fade and requires a proactive effort from Wilberforce and the Parochial Church Council. Members of the congregation share my empathy for Ivee, inwardly, however peer pressure is holding them back from showing their feelings publicly.

Ivee skipped into the hall like an eager energetic puppy and proclaimed, "here's the flowers. Are they okay? Daffodils are little droopy, but the tulips and bluebells are beautiful."

"Where did you find them?" I asked abruptly without thanking her for the effort and acknowledging her initiative however this was the aspect troubling me. Ivee's smile shone brightly, and she replied, "I picked them from the gardens."

"Which gardens?" My interrogation continued without consideration.

"In front of the small cottage next to the Vicarage and by the side of the large bungalow with the red door. The white picket fence is amazing!" Ivee seemed oblivious to my ever-growing concern, but her youthful enthusiasm sometimes overtakes a sensible assessment.

"Thank God!" My booming voice reverberated throughout the hall and was as much as a surprise to me as to the fellow volunteers. Ivee's face contorted with worry, "I'm so sorry. I thought in a small village everyone likes to join in with the celebrations for St. George's Day. They looked so pretty and were by the fence."

Before I had a chance to make amends for my startled reaction Molly chipped in with a curt comment, "No good standing around gossiping, we can't stick them back. Let's get into the kitchen. Sandwiches won't be making themselves."

I stared at Molly however she was oblivious to my stern facial expression. The priority was the work in the kitchen, and she firmly believes taking a tough line with Ivee will not do her any harm in fact quite the opposite. I took a deep breath and made a mental note to apologise to Revd James Wiggett and Basil Bloome for the incursion into their private gardens. Hopefully, their status in the community, that is, the retired vicar and a member of the Parochial Church Council will soften their reaction.

Hannah, weighed down with bags, tripped over the loose paving step by the entrance. Mervyn instinctively reached out to steady her and offered to carry the excess luggage. "Do you think this will be enough?" she asked. "Wil did not know how many to expect. Hopefully will be a full house or should I say hall. Nice chance to meet more people in the village."

I looked at the vicar's wife with pity in my heart but did not verbalise my fear because it would be far too patronising. '*She really does not know what she has let herself in for*,' I thought.

Hannah reshaped her ditsy print, button detail, midi tea dress and said, "I saw Ivee in Revd Wiggett's garden. She is kind but didn't know the care rota had been agreed? Just a bit worried because he does get quite agitated if he doesn't know in advance."

"Long story," I replied, "Ivee is extremely excited and enthusiastic about helping today. I'll have a chat with her later."

Hillary Sheppard, the associate vicar, is a techie whizz: already updating the website and even trying to introduce an app. The idea is falling on rocky ground. His Faith is strong even in the world of '*anti-social media.*' A term I use borne out of sheer frustration of trying to have a conversation when others have a mobile device stuck in front of their face. Old age is tiresome however I am eternally thankful that I experienced life without the internet, laptops, and mobile phones. Simple and sociable. Hillary adjusted the microphone for the vicar and after a few false starts the words of welcome echoed throughout the hall. There was a fair turn out and everyone enjoyed the music arranged by Hillary. He told me he used something called '*Spotifly?*' Couldn't hear or understand his explanation. I must learn to keep up with the changes in technology although there seems to be new versions each month and of course each upgrade costs more.

"Has Bernadette arrived?" Hannah asked.

Molly replied before I could put my cup down. "She'll be still doing her hair and fixing the make-up." I quickly intervened, "I'll call her to see how she is getting on." Hannah's anxiety was increasing because Bernadette had promised to bring the prizes for the raffle.

Bernadette Bunting has the looks and appearance of the iconic actress Betty Davis. Bernadette does not enjoy being a spinster especially when new members of the congregation announce their engagement with elation and expect us to join in with their celebration. The successful career as an Executive Assistant for Flinuse PLC, a Life Assurance company in Basingstoke, and her chocolate box cottage on the outskirts of the village and the abundance of disposable income does not fill the gap in her life which darkens her days. Bernadette's recent return from the walk in the wilderness of agnosticism is causing more angst. Hannah is offering support, but Bernadette is still hiding behind the brick wall of self-pity. I want to maintain the friendship with Bernadette however can no longer tolerate her monologues. Perseverance in the restoration of patience is high on my prayer list, but mum keeps reminding me, '*Just because we are Christians, we are not door mats.*'

***

"IVEE!" Molly called out. "Start collecting the cups, the trays are in the kitchen, by the sink. Scarlet will help ye if your glasses are steamed up."

Scarlet Chortle is one of the Church Wardens. A disciplined character which extends to her clothing which is more like a uniform i.e., the same outfit is worn on the same day each week. Checked pleated skirts in various shades appear frequently coupled with lambswool jumpers and crepe blouses with a frilled edge collar during warmer weather. A vast range of silk scarves shine brightly under her natural curly ginger hair which is the only unkempt part of her appearance. She has taken on the vocation of volunteering following her retirement as a Librarian. The idea of a Book Club was muted but there was no progress nor appetite for a literary gathering. Scarlet, in her role as Chair of the Social

Club committee, included the proposal on the notes filed in a handmade leather document holder – a family heirloom. The zipped wallet holds the fountain pens and green blotting paper and is stored securely in the brown corner cupboard situated in the hall by the cracked window.

The hubbub emanating from the kitchen was increasing due to Molly's frustration at Ivee's slow pace and giggling with Hillary Sheppard, the associate vicar. I caused a distraction by dropping the tablecloth I was twisting into a strange shape which will cause all sorts of problems at the next community lunch.

"Hillary, can you help please?" I nudged his elbow encouraging him to turn away from Ivee whose smile beamed as wide as a Cheshire cat.

He blushed and replied, "yes, of course, what shall I do?"

"Thank you," I accepted his offer with relief. "Okay, think we need to start from scratch. Let's take the four corners. I used to help my mum fold the sheets, there is a special technique and definitely needs two people."

Folding sheets was an alien concept to Hillary. His blank expression showcased the confusion as to why people spend time carrying out this task. Duvets just need to be shaken in the air. I cannot begin to imagine how baffled he would be if I introduced candy stripe flannelette sheets into the conversation. Instead, I asked if he was looking forward to meeting the exchange student.

"Yes, it'll be great. He is staying at the Vicarage; we might have to share the annexe if my rental agreement is not complete before June. I can't remember his name, how annoying, Ivee just told me. Ah! That's it – Johannes."

"Where is he from?" I asked.

"Norway," Hillary replied as quick as a flash and his excitement escalated. "Amazing! Imagine living there. Scandinavia is stunning. Is that correct region? Three countries - Norway, Sweden and uhm?" I interjected, "Denmark."

Hillary smiled and said, "Please be on my Quiz team. Wilberforce has asked me to organise a Quiz. Not sure where to start but Ivee's volunteered to help, and Lester goes to the Quiz nights at The Old Door Inn. It'll be all right on the night if it is at night. I don't think Logan will like us being in the hall after dark. There's a wide range of knowledge in the church." He took a deep breath and continued, "I am sorry. I ramble on when nervous."

Tear drops dampened the sides of my cheek, and I blew my nose. "Don't worry." I said reassuringly. "it's not catching. Hay Fever!"

Ivee scurried out from the kitchen to ask if we needed an extra pair of hands. Hillary's protracted and exaggerated laugh rang alarm bells in my head, and I observed the lines on the vicar's forehead tighten with dread.

"Thank you, Ivee, but we're okay aren't we Hillary?" He nodded in compliance with my prompt. "Best check if Molly needs help." My suggestion was followed by an invitation, "when you're finished in the kitchen, would you like to go for a hot chocolate?" Ivee's eyes widened and her face lit up, "Wow! That'll be amazing."

I discreetly exchanged a look of relief and realisation with Wilberforce Trent – the new vicar, juggling lots of different responsibilities. He does not want a scandal in the parish especially with a new recruit. I do not want Ivee to experience a broken heart. The fractured emotion is inevitable in life however need to mentor her during the early stage of her career and protect her from the prying eyes waiting for her to trip up so they can proclaim their concerns were justified.

***

CHAPTER 3

"Only me!" I called out and pressed the front doorbell.

"Where's your key?" my mum asked.

"At home with my trainers. My feet hurt – they're throbbing! Haven't got the energy to get them."

Mum gave me a hug and then nudged my arm, "silly Blodwyn, I'll get you a tea; dinner won't be long."

I sunk into the extra-large flowery armchair in the front room. The softness soothed my aching joints, but my feet expanded as I tugged at the blue court shoes which were embedded solidly into my ankles. I chuckled quietly when mum reverted to her Welsh roots when referring to me at as a '*silly Blodwyn - flower*.' My brother, Gareth never connected to Wales, and it was not clear why, however he proudly named his eldest child, Cedwyn, much to mum's delight. I don't think Gareth looked into the history of Saint Cedwyn because he is a doubtful Christian. We went to the Church of England schools because we were told to, not out of choice, as did all children in our generation. Gareth tried to hide his relief when he went to University in Bristol, but the signs were written all over his face. Mum's thoughts were blurred by her worry about the temptations in the student accommodation. Gareth liked a few beers with his friends and a game of pool and tenpin bowling, but all-night parties were not on his timetable. When he had enough money saved, he enjoyed going to rugby matches. We did not have money on tap from our parents. "Me and your father are not walking cash machines." Mum used to say when we tried to get spending money from dad or should I say, "*when I tried to ask dad for money*." Part time work and regular deposits into piggy banks accrued interest – not financial but my curiosity. I tried to convince mum I had accidentally dropped the ceramic piggy bank but that did not wash. "I was only trying to put the black thingy (i.e., small round bendable plastic seal) back!" My appeal was rejected, and my coins were relegated to an old red 'Elastoplast' elastic adhesive bandage tin: not pretty like my cute girly piggy bank with rosy cheeks with flowers and a blue bow on the head. Gareth methodically kept his savings in the tin plate 'treasure chest' money box. The black red and gold patterns on the lid ignited my imagination of pirates hiding gold and maps. Unfortunately, when I picked up the tin using the handle on the lid, the coins rattled, triggering a noise which mum tuned into no matter where she was in the house. "RUTH!" she ordered, "Leave your brother's tin alone! "When my rebellious streak rose to the surface I complained, "But Mum! I was only looking." Mum's response was firm and final, "go and look in your bedroom and put your books back on the shelf." I complied with the instruction. There was no intention to take money and even if I did want to take an interest free loan it was an impossible venture because Gareth kept the key with him.

I had a stable and secure upbringing, interspersed with disharmony like most families even within the church family. The common perception of a congregation is - people going to church services wearing halos, open toed sandals and carrying an oversized leather-bound bible. Whereas they carry emotional baggage and wear jumpers, that is, until the boiler is repaired. Their woes and fears are alleviated by prayer and fellowship. Mum and Dad have lived in the same house in Old Botlean since they were married in 1965. Conversation about downsizing concluded with a commitment not to move. Mum said she could not imagine calling anywhere else home. She is a sprightly 73-year-old, maintaining high standards in her role as house manager and a devout member of the community although resigned from being the Chair of the Residents' Association last year. "Stronger youthful energy is needed," she said reluctantly. The members empathised with the circumstances, but the timing matched the need for exuberant stamina, to challenge the authorities with regards the pace of change in the village.

"There you go, sleepy head," Mum said softly, "please don't knock the cup over, the carpets were cleaned yesterday. I yawned and shook my head to encourage my eye lids to open fully and engage my brain with my curiosity. "Which company did you choose?" Mum picked up '*my mug*' with the letters R and B intertwined – painted in hand illustrated watercolour flowers with a hint of gold. R is for Ruth and B is for Brigitta – my middle name chosen because mum's favourite film is the Sound of Music. I most certainly do not share the character's musicality however share the personality traits of independence and enjoyment of reading but do not possess such a forthright approach when expressing my opinions. I do suffer from '*foot in mouth disease*' which gets me into awkward corners and concede it causes upset. It remains a mystery how mum knew the choice of Brigitta would match my character. Women's intuition? More like, mum's insight into how I inherited some of her characteristics because Gareth shared dad's looks and temperament.

***

"C.C. Botlean."

I looked quizzically at mum and said, "sorry?" Mum smiled sympathetically, "you're not with it, are you? The name of the carpet cleaning company. Declan recommended them. They're great; so friendly and hardworking. I'll give you their number. Your carpets need a refresh." I pushed my hair back over my ears and stretched my arms in the air.

Declan Regal is the Landlord of The Old Door Inn. A good old-fashioned pub and a de facto community centre. He has managed the pub with his wife, Penny, for twenty years. The New Year Eve's Party welcoming in the new millennium was an enormous success and integrated them into the community. Memories and pictures will last a lifetime and is still the highlight of conversations each Christmas. Declan started offering free lunches on Christmas Day in 2008. The financial crisis in that year crushed lives so the seasonal selfless act of Christian giving was a blessing. Declan and Penny are not regular church goers however generously contribute towards the community lunches. The Old Door Inn hosts different events: the quiz night is the most popular and has kept its regular Monday evening slot. The Karaoke night was not a crowd pleaser. Rumour has it that my dad had a good try at singing, '*Green, Green Grass of Home.*' Thankfully, no one recorded the first and last attempt and Sir Tom Jones will never be subjected to this particularly unusual version of the song. I have been told there was also dad dancing but do not even want to think about that. Fortunately, I was living in London so was spared the embarrassment however the performance is recorded in Old Botlean folklore. The '*Talent in OB Night*' re-branded as '*Toby Night*' attracted a crowd initially, but a shortage of local contestants and allegations of biased judges resulted in the removal of the event from the social calendar. The Sunday roast dinners are delicious but are no competition for my mum's roasts which are legendary. She is blessed with cooking skills which have not been passed down to me.

After my spell of yawning accompanied by strange clicking sounds in my cheeks. I asked, "what's for dinner?" Mum closed the top oven door with slightly more force than usual, "Shepherd's pie. We should be having roast beef, but dad insisted.

I tried to put forward a case to support dad, "it's his favourite."

Mum huffed, "he said he'll be back at 5." Assume Trevor's buying him just one more whiskey. I smiled to ease her worry and offered to cut up the broccoli as a form of distraction. "I'll call him." "No point," mum said sharply. "His mobile is not as mobile as he is. It's on the sideboard. Mind you, not much good if had taken it – he turns it off when in the club house."

"They'll have to get a taxi," I said wondering if the extended delay would cause the pressure in the kitchen to rise. "No," mum replied indignantly, Miss Chalk will jump at the chance at playing chauffeur. Showing off their new car."

"Mum! Put your claws away. Trevor is married to Angie now, so she is Mrs Teacher. If you accept what's happened, it'll be easier for everyone, especially dad." Mum frowned and shared her outrage for the umpteenth time. "What on earth got into him? Angela did everything for him. She adored him, think she still does, poor woman. Then, THEN! He finds Miss Supermodel more like Miss Superficial. Such a waste! Thank God they didn't have children. Dad has invited Trevor to dinner on Friday!" I mumbled, "should be a fun evening."

"Angela is my friend and can have a normal conversation with her. What am I going to say to the new Mrs Teacher? Latest gossip about Lust Island!" I chuckled and corrected mum. "Love Island." She knows the name but would never admit to watching the clips on TV. Her catty remarks are rooted in worry for Angela Teacher because she has never lived alone and fall out from such a devastating blow can take time to surface. "Vegan!" Mum carped on, "what do I cook? "I replied sheepishly, "you can ask her."

The muscles on mum's lower jaw tightened with frustration and said, "I'm not cooking three or four different dishes just to please that woman." Mum liked to cook one meal not an array of dishes. We sat down at the table and enjoyed the food and family time without distractions. Mobiles, telephone, and television were turned off. Nan used to say, "whoever eats together stays together." I used to laugh at her but as time goes on, I have learnt to respect her wise words.

Mum flicked through the pages of the latest cookbook added to the pine wooden shelves above the cream marble work surface closest to the kitchen window. Well, if dad moans about tofu or quinoa or whatever you call it, then he can moan at Trevor."

When mum had a rant, she didn't hold back. Best to get it out her system now rather than in front of Trevor and Angie. Trevor Teacher succumbed to the temptation of a middle age crisis. New clothes and a new wife after thirty years of marriage. Angie Teacher (nee Chalk) was born in 1989 – thirty years after Trevor. She is a stunning blonde haired, blue eyed, arm candy. lanky is a harsh description but think she eats one lettuce leaf a day. Membership to Champneys Forest Mere spa resort in Liphook, a rural Hampshire village in the South Downs, must be the secret.

Angie resigned from her role as a Personal Assistant to Trevor once his divorce was finalised therefore the cliché of the affair with the secretary claimed another victim. Trevor Teacher inherited a vast sum from his Great Aunty Edna who he did not see much but she adored him and being a spinster, he inherited her entire Estate. He gave money to

Edna's private carers who worked tirelessly to ensure she was not put into a care home - her last wish. His ex-wife, Angela, kept their family home. Trevor was not interested in the tired house. He bought a new detached house with a garage for his new car – a Jaguar. Angie had free reign to decorate their spacious home with all the trendy designs you only see in magazines. Who lives in homes without a hint of dust nor a crumb on the floor? Someone in the house must eat a biscuit.

Trevor first met dad at the golf club in Hook, Hampshire. They enjoyed a relaxed friendship despite their age difference. Although the weight of awkwardness after his divorce has put a strain on their relationship dad feels sorry for Trevor. We couldn't pinpoint a moment when he changed from a loyal husband to a rebel trying to relieve his youth which he never had. Trevor was not a lady's man, not fashionable and not interested in sporty cars. His grey ford fiesta suited his character. "Just a convenience to get from A to B," he used to say. Trevor retired early because the inherited investments provide a comfortable income although we are not sure what will happen if Angie has children, and her appetite increases for spending her husband's money. Mum repeatedly advised him to arrange a prenuptial agreement, but the words fell on deaf ears. Dad was far too embarrassed to get involved in the conversation. "He'll regret it," mum said, "she'll take him to the cleaners and back!"

"Do you want your pudding now?" Mum asked enthusiastically.

I tugged at the waist band of my skirt and sighed, "not at moment, I'm full. Shepherd's pie was super!" Dad sniggered and mimicked my expression, "super!?" I gave a whimper in protest, "Daa.d! Stop, I'm too tired." Mum intervened, "I'll put your bread-and-butter pudding in your takeaway bowl and give you a jug of custard. Better than packet of powder you've got in your cupboard, even if it is instant!"

"Thanks mum." I replied softly. She continued with the plans for my evening, "I'll drive you home. Dad has had a few drinks with his friends." Mum's tone made the words sound like a '*telling off*' but their marriage of fifty-four years withstood banter because it was good natured – not spiteful and it was not one-sided. Dad would give as good as he got but mastered the skill of delivering his punch lines at the right times e.g., most definitely not when they are with Angie Teacher. Mum and dad are a united team. Occasionally I heard heated discussions, however peace was restored quickly. Another one of Nan's sayings was, "don't go to bed on an argument." Dad kept to this pearl of wisdom from his mother-in-law. Mum did not always follow the advice and held on to grievances for a couple of days. Regrettably, I held on to hurt and disagreements too long. It does not damage the other person. The only one damaged is me. I am getting better but slip up now and then. I often wonder if I can change.

"Ouch!" I cried out as the blister on my ankle burned. I limped towards the front door. "Where's your shoes?" Mum went through the departure check list which was irritating but efficient. I groaned, "can't get them back on!"

"Use my slippers," Mum replied with empathy topped with a dusting of a lecture which will be delegated to dad to present their concern about the disproportionate time spent volunteering in comparison to the other members of the congregation.

Dad offered a solution. "Use mine. A '*super*' Christmas present from your Nan; handmade in Wales. Just right for your chunky feet.!

I replied with a grin and grimace etched on my face, "thanks dad. Love you too!"

Dad said, "take care of yourself. Working too many hours at the church. You're only meant to be part time?" Dad put his arm around my shoulder, and I drew comfort and strength from his protective gesture. I tried to explain using a mixture of excuses. "I know! I know! But poor

Wilberforce. He really has been thrown in the deep end. Helping until him and Hannah settle in. She looks exhausted and they've got two children."

"No buts!" Dad replied. "They've got two daughters who are old enough to help and plenty of volunteers They are both young and fighting fit ready for the battle against the doubters."

I looked down at my feet which were alarmingly spreading by the minute and said, "Yeah, but. "Dad interjected. "No buts!" I laughed and continued, "the volunteers are, let's say more mature and a bit rusty."

"Cheek!" Mum blurted out and struck back. "I'm not rusty, a bit slower, but not rusty!"

Dad intervened, "oh, Gladys, you know she doesn't mean any harm. She can hardly keep her eyes open."

"If you say so." Mum turned away in a huff and then started packing me up to leave. "Come on Blodwyn, let's get you settled in for the night. Have you got milk?" I yawned and sighed, "little bit." "I've ordered from the milkman, Be alright until morning." Mum shuffled along the hall and called out, "wait, I'll get you a pint from the fridge."

Dad's expression turned to a serious complexion which was a warning of the words to come. He rubbed my arm. "You need to slow down. I know you like to help but you're no good to anyone if you are unwell. Your mum is worried but…" Before he had the chance to finish, I jumped in to say, "No buts! Dad." He laughed and conceded, "okay, you win this time but I'm not throwing the towel in yet."

Mum provided an update on progress. "I've put bread, bananas and honey in the bag with the milk." Dad replied with a mix of impatience and logic, "she's not going on a picnic. She'll be asleep as soon as she sees the bed." Dad helped pack the car and said, "are you coming for Sunday roast?" I replied with restored vigour. "Try and stop me!"

***

CHAPTER 4

"GREEN!" Mrs Redbridge snapped.

Mrs Sharpe scowled and retorted, "NO! The minutes clearly show the door will be painted blue. We had a vote. The vicar will tell you. Won't you?" All the members of the Parochial Church Council (PCC) stared at the vicar awaiting to hear the adjudication. The interlude hung in the air and the ticking of the clock in the church hall amplified the anticipation.

"Now, now, ladies. Let's stop for a moment and take a breath." Wilberforce looked at me and shook his head slowly and discretely. I took the signal to mean the curt exchange should not be included in the minutes. I thought, '*no wonder Naomi didn't want to do the minutes today.*' In my eagerness to help I volunteered to be the secretary for the PCC meeting on Thursday 26th April. The vicar continued his peace mission, "I acknowledge the colour of the door is a valuable contribution to welcome new visitors and we need to listen to each person's opinion however, regrettably, time is against us.

Wilberforce shuffled his papers and said hesitantly, "we will move onto the report from John. Please go ahead."

John Eton is the Treasurer. A sombre character both by nature and choice of clothing. We think he has a wardrobe full of grey trousers and V-neck jumpers and twill grid, cobalt blue check shirts, because this is the same daily costume. The garments look pristine, trousers ironed with a sharp edge which must take a lot of time and concentration. He has the ideal qualities for the role which he took on in January 2019 after Rev Wiggett retired. Speculation threaded its way through the village as to the timing. "The Vicar did not like him from the moment he saw him," said Mrs Redbridge with a level of authority and hint of insider information. "Think the feeling was mutual," said another member of the PCC - Basil Bloome, as he jumped on the rumour wheel.

The cups rattled as they leaned precariously on the edge of the tray carried by Ivee Chong. "You are not supposed to be here!" screeched Mrs Redbridge. "For goodness' sake," said Mrs Sharpe as she leapt up to catch one cup before it hit the table. "You'll scare the life out of her. She's only bringing tea and biscuits. We're not talking about any top-secret plans, and even if we were, you can get her to sign a non-disclosure agreement." The quest to catch the cup was unsuccessful. Slivers of the broken ceramic cup intermingled with the papers on the table. "I'm so sorry," Ivee cried.

"Please forgive me. Sorry, sorry!" I approached Ivee slowly by skimming my feet across the surface of the floor instead of taking sharp steps. I fixed my focus on the teapot decorated with painted daffodils and filled to the brim with boiling hot water. "It's all okay Ivee," I smiled softly and said quietly, "please stand still, I will take the tray." I managed to loosen Ivee's grip and took the tray to a table in the corner near the broken window? My sigh of relief extended further than intended.

"I am so sorry," Ivee gasped and rambled on, "I'll get a cloth and brush and rubbish bag and new cups." Ivee was shaking and I reached out to hold her hand and said, "thank you for offering. We will be okay. Humphrey will be delighted to get our tea and biscuits. He knows where the secret stash of chocolate fingers is kept. Don't you Humphrey?"

Humphrey Crook, is a member of the PCC and has been a Church Warden for five years, nodded and winked. Humphrey is a bubbly character with a sparkle of eccentricity which makes him even more endearing. The remaining wisps of white curly hair settle on his shirt collar. Humphrey does not wear tee-shirts. He is entangled in a web of confusion as to the meaning and purpose of '*casual clothes*.'

"If you're looking for Hillary, he's in the church on cleaning duty," said Mrs Redbridge in a mischievous manner before she delivered the punchline. "I'm sure he will be over the moon to have you by his side." There was no laughter not even a polite chuckle. Mrs Sharpe broke through the wall of silence, "please can you just stop! Leave the poor girl alone."

Scarlet Chortle, a member of the PCC and a Church Warden, offered a compromise. "Ivee, come back in one hour and you can help me in the kitchen. You know, just as you did on Tuesday?" Ivee nodded in recognition of the offer to redeem herself and scuttled off towards the church. Scarlett's content expression was reinforced once she had straightened her navy checked pleated skirt accompanied by a navy boucle jacket, which was not on the Thursday uniform rota - an exception for the PCC meeting. Her crisp white crepe blouse with a frilled edge collar restored the balance and discipline of the outfit schedule.

Wilberforce tapped his pen on the table to restore order. "Okay, thank you everyone. Please may I request everyone is patient with Ivee. She has made a good start as the Children & Families Minister. It is a new position we have introduced to help reach out to the community and support our Christian family. "There is a lot to do and a lot to learn."

"Hope she is learning to stay out of my garden," Basil quipped.

"Oh Basil," Mrs Sharpe muttered. "Ivee has apologised and so has the Vicar. She won't be flower arranging again unless you need help with your garden." Basil replied instantaneously, "it's not the flower arranging but the flower picking that is worrying."

Krystal Sharpe is forty-two years of age and the newest member of the PCC. Her age and inexperience weighs against her in such an '*old church clique*.' Wilberforce's aim is to create more relaxed meetings and introduce more diversity. One of the many daunting tasks he must face whilst dodging the doubters who are coming at him from every angle.

John Eton resumed sharing his presentation and the members listened intently with the odd amusing acknowledgement by Humphrey when looking at the pie charts in an assortment of colours. The estimated cost for the repairs is eye-watering. Wilberforce digested the figures and lifted his head ashen faced. The enormity of the issue was soon drowned out by another squabble. This time, about the collection plate. Scarlet Chortle put forward her comment without invitation, "I asked Reverend Wiggett on more than one occasion about changing to a collection bag." John replied and shared the next part of his presentation with trepidation. "The records show there are discrepancies with the total amount shown on the entry book for collections after Sunday services and the relevant weekly bank account stamped deposit slips. Please do not take this as a criticism, I am sure these are only human errors. We all slip up at times." Basil looked extremely troubled and asked, "how many slips are we talking about exactly?" John coughed and gulped loudly before replying. "Twenty-two." A mixture of embarrassment and bewilderment formatted the reaction. "Oh my," said Humphrey, "I used to count the collections once a month so twelve of the mistakes could be my fault?"

Mrs Redbridge slapped the top of the table with her right hand and declared in a high-pitched voice, "it is definitely not my fault! I used to make entries split by the different coins and notes collected and filled out the paying in slip. The totals always matched. Naomi promised to leave the keys to the office in the old tea caddy, but she forgot most weeks. She's never been the same after her divorce."

Naomi Zamberletti's ex-husband, Paulo, left her for a family friend aged twenty-two. Youthfulness was no doubt an attraction for him however the fact she was not a Christian seemed to be a major pull factor. Paulo was raised in a strict Roman Catholic home and ironically it turned him off religion. Paulo proudly pronounced his girlfriend was expecting their first child before the divorce was finalised. A double betrayal because he declared he never wanted children. Naomi was acutely aware of the comments in people's mind and on their lips. "*I told you, didn't I? I knew he wanted children but not with her.*" At the age of thirty-eight, Naomi is cautiously optimistic she will have a baby. I cannot begin to imagine how long it will take to recover from such callousness and cowardice. Paulo lives in London which is a small mercy amidst the heart ache. Although there is a distance in physical miles the bind by social media is tightening because Naomi cannot cut the last piece of thread. She is obsessed with looking at the images of the blooming pregnancy.

John tried to veer the conversation from accusation to how they need to manage the accounting process in future. "No one person is at fault. It is our collective responsibility to be good stewards so we will have to start new procedures; for example, two people to count the collection together and there will be a safe in the Vicarage if we cannot find the office key. I will set out other guidelines in a report which will be handed out at the next PCC meeting. I appreciate the time allocated to this topic." Wilberforce almost looked relieved there were no further financial announcements today. "Thank you, John. You have invested a lot of time on the audit and preparing your presentation. Okay, is there any other business?" Krystal replied, "Yes. I can make enquiries about obtaining a card machine. We can leave the card reader by the church door to reduce the risk managing the cash donations." Mrs Redbridge cut in before Wilberforce had the chance to open his mouth. "Most of us will not know how to use it. Someone will have to stand by the machine to show them what to do. There are no plug sockets by the door, and the old wiring falling off the wall will electrocute someone soon. Suppose someone steals the machine. What do we do then?"

"Thank you, Mrs Redbridge," Wilberforce said wearily. "We are going to have a short break before our guest speaker joins us." Timothy Carpenter, the local Councillor, knocked on the door and took one step inside the hall. "Hello, welcome," said a re-energised Wilberforce. "Come and join us. We don't bite, well not all the time."

"That is Ethel's chair!" Mrs Redbridge's cutting opening line struck fear onto Timothy's face. "Oh, I am sorry. Will she be arriving soon?"

"I sincerely hope not, "said Basil with a sarcastic tone lingering on his tongue. "Ethel died five years ago. Takes a while for Mrs Redbridge to absorb change." Doris glared at Basil and wanted to give him a piece of her mind but was mindful of the Vicar and how she did not want to lose her prestigious role. "You could have said, passed away," She protested petulantly.

Doris went to school with Ethel and misses her friendship. Although married, Doris feels lonely. Bill, her husband, is committed to the institution of marriage rather than to Doris. Bill Redbridge works in the Council Office in Basingstoke. The promotion to a Senior Officer in the team managing Council Tax fulfilled Bill's rather restricted career ambition. He is happy with routine and his dedicated wife. He has not or will not cheat on Doris because of the hassle that would ensue. Adultery is locked in his mind. Doris can see the distance in his eyes and accepts the status quo. Lunches, afternoon teas and knitting days with Ethel were an escapism and a comfort. Doris will not upset the apple cart. Bill's pension from the Council will start next year on his 65th birthday. A milestone they are both looking forward to. Doris is already looking at cruise brochures however the idea does not match Bill's vision of a more sedate retirement. "I just want to put my feet up in my home." Not to mention how he suffered with sea sickness during the trip to Normandy organised by the men in the congregation."

***

CHAPTER 5

Water boiled over onto the stainless-steel gas hob. "NO!" I blurted out and grabbed the extremely hot handle of the saucepan. "OUCH!"

"Do you need a hand?" Geraldine asked and tried to stifle her laughter.

"Am I glad to see you!"

"You're always glad to see me." Geraldine chortled.

The friendship I share with Geraldine is a precious gift and the longevity is rare. Our first interaction in the nursery class involved my outburst of tears falling into the play sandpit, causing a terrible mess, and Geraldine announcing with glee, "apple crumble pudding today." Geraldine is well rounded; her description not mine. I think she is a yummy mummy Her three children, Eógan aged fifteen, Padraig aged thirteen and Siobhán aged 10, are the best free fitness class. Her husband, Seamus O'Connell, is a successful marketing director but happily slots into place under the management of Geraldine with regards plans for their home and children. Seamus trusts her implicitly. PDAs (public display of affection) is not their bag; her description not mine. Their mutual deep love and respect is usually covered up with that unique Irish humour which many try to replicate but inhibition closes the safety curtain over their act. Seamus gave a cracking speech on their wedding day, including the line, "my missus is a jewel, God was looking down on me when she came into my sight." Geraldine heckled her husband, "I was just looking into your wallet!" Howls of laughter rose above the decorations in the church hall. Happiness intertwined in the hearts of the beautiful bride and groom.

I perused the brown sticky mess at the bottom of the saucepan, "well, peas are off the menu." "Mushy peas," Geraldine replied. "You must have a tin of mushy peas at the back of your cupboard? I'm not going to be defeated by a burnt pan of peas! But you'll have to put a new saucepan on your birthday list. There's no way you're going to remove those stubborn stains no matter how many Mr Muscles you've got in your kitchen!"

Geraldine's rhetorical question, "sitting with trays?" was acknowledged with a nod and a statement that I knew would be met with a protest and rebellion. "Mobiles off!"

"WHAT!?!" Geraldine tried to look astounded. We went through the same routine when she came to my house for a meal. "You know what I'm going to say and I'm not going to change my mind no matter how much you pretend to be upset and pull a pouty face. I want to talk to you without beeps going off every five minutes."

"You are such a grouch!" Geraldine retorted before asking, "where's the vinegar?"

"Usual place." I replied and shuffled on the armchair to balance the tray. I love a fish and chip supper especially when shared with my dear friend. The fish is not fried due to my over sensitive stomach which is such a shame. Oven baked is a fair compromise and saves me taking a loads of indigestion tablets throughout the night and the next day. The smelly breath is escalating and increasingly embarrassing so need to reduce the acid reflux as much as possible. Getting old is not much fun but has some advantages, for example, uhmm..I am unable to think of any at the moment but will be eternally grateful I was alive when our lives were not ruled by the internet and mobiles. If someone told me when I was ten that we would be carrying around phones which can take photos, can access our bank accounts, e-mails and watch Strictly Come Dancing I would have laughed at them. The mobiles have moved from our bags to our hands, to the dinner tables, to our faces, when family and friends are trying to have a conversation. My line of thought was interrupted.

"There'll be on their second pizza by now!"

"Is Seamus looking after all of them?" I enquired concerned about the consequences. He does not have much experience of looking after their three children when altogether.

"Yeah." Geraldine seemed to be more relaxed than me but as a masterful mum she knew what to expect and how to clean up the pieces in the morning. "There'll be spoilt rotten. Seamus promised them pizza, popcorn, and cinema night on the TV. No doubt Eógan and Padraig will be in their rooms playing Fourweeks? Or something like that: can't keep up with all these games. Siobhán will be sitting with daddy talking him into buying the next new toy or gadget or princess dress. He promised me he will not be working on his laptop. I told him I'll check up on him. Siobhán is CCTV on legs; she sees and hears everything."

I proffered advice which I sensed would go down like a lead balloon, "you can get those systems where you can block internet access. Why don't you ask about that? Worth a try."

"Could give it a go!" Geraldine replied. "I'll have a look on the internet – excuse the pun."

Geraldine had children later in life. Partially due to trying to find a suitable stage in her husband's career but in large part due to lack of confidence installed by Seamus' mother. She didn't approve of Geraldine from the start. Her comments hurt Geraldine and deterred her from having children for many years. Bernadette wanted her son to marry a local girl. Local to Dublin not local to London. Seamus always wanted a daughter. Geraldine just prayed all her children would be healthy. Their daughter was born in 2009 when Geraldine was forty. They baptised her Siobhán: the name means God is gracious.

My stare transfixed on the delightful painting on the wall above the fireplace. The portrait captured the spectacular Møns Klint. Chalk cliffs gently crumble into the Baltic Sea on the island of Møn, located about two hours south of Copenhagen. My darling husband's artistry told the story of how much he loved one of the most famous and beautiful places in Denmark. He never tired looking at or talking about the abundance of unique flora and fauna associated with the area. He encouraged me to experience the Maglevand stairs at Geocenter Møns Klint, from the top of the cliff down to the beach. I was exhausted but elated to create the memory in one of my all too rare visits to his homeland. On the mantelpiece was a photo taken on our wedding day held securely in a solid silver frame. My mother was none too pleased with my demure Maggie embroidered ivory dress. She tolerated my fashion choice but put her foot down forcefully when it came to the venue for the reception. The church hall was not even on her radar. Mum arranged and dad paid for the celebration in Tylney Hall. A stunning venue. The Master Suite was magnificent for our first night as a married couple, indeed our first night together. I made foolish mistakes in the past but wanted my relationship with Peder to be special and it was more than I can express in words. We were overwhelmed with the opulence but more so the expense because our budget could not stretch to cover the cost of such luxury. We had a heavenly honeymoon in Denmark which involved a small celebration with his mother and a few of his relatives. His mother thought he was a confirmed bachelor and did not want her only child to move to England, but Peder wanted to break free from the weight of expectation.

Peder was a '*Free Spirit*' – his words not mine. He had travelled many miles and fulfilled his ambition of being an artist. We met in the National Art Gallery in London. I nearly knocked into one of the paintings with my rucksack, and he kindly explained it was not a good idea to scratch a painting by Vincent van Gogh, because it may be quite expensive to repair. After I gasped and laughed, Peder provided an insightful interpretation of the painting. He bought me a bunch of sunflowers on our first date to commemorate the meaning of our meeting. The twenty-year age gap caused both mothers to be worried, but I was not troubled nor noticed that Peder was older than me. Of course, mum raised the topic about Peder's lack of wealth. She subtly, no, with brutal honesty asked me to draw up a pre-nuptial agreement just in case he claimed half of my house. I refused which resulted in a few weeks of the silent treatment, but dad persuaded her it will be all fine and was brave enough to mention they did not have a pre-nuptial agreement and they were okay. He must of have had a double brandy before making such an inflammatory statement. In the end there was no need for any of the worry. Peder never asked for money and would never have taken any of my possessions. He stole my heart and although our time together was far too brief, I thank God each day, I met him. My trip down memory lane was abruptly diverted to the suggestion loudly announced by Geraldine. "You got to get back out there – on the market again."

"I'm not a farm animal going to market," I replied.

"Might be a good idea, should get a fair price but not for breeding. Past that post." Geraldine's suggestion prompted my quip. "Cheers! That's made me feel a lot better! Anyway, you were fifty in March. You're three months older than me."

"Older and wiser," Geraldine said. "Like mature wine we get better with age."

I laughed and admitted, "I feel like a flat fizzy drink. No matter how many times I shake the bottle the bubbles do not come back."

Geraldine hit the nail on the head, "in plain English – you're feeling old and haggard?"

"Yep!" I agreed with Geraldine's diagnosis but did not agree with the next idea, "You need a date night. How about Lester? Nice man. Home above the shop or should I say Post Office. And he brings flowers. Have you found out who the lucky lady is? Could be a man?"

I struggle, at times, to keep up with Geraldine when she is in warp speed – equal to the speed of light. I recalled an insight into Lester's mysterious private life. "Mum remembers him going out with, uhm, what's her name?"

Geraldine looked confused. "You'll have to give me a better clue."

"You know," I said. "One from greengrocers. Started with L?"

"Lettuce?" Geraldine chuckled.

"Ha! Ha!" I replied. "You should sign up for the next talent night."

Geraldine smiled, "Is that still going? Thought Penny was going to cancel it. Totally cringeworthy and painful to watch. I think they should bring back the karaoke."

I blurted an abstract comment, "Melanie! Knew I'd remember. Takes a while but get there in the end."

"Melanie?" Geraldine asked, "who's she?"

"Lady from the greengrocers. Keep up! You need your ears tested. I miss the greengrocers. So much change. Be nothing left soon. Christine is just about clinging onto the hairdressers. She can't afford to keep the Saturday girl on."

"She must earn a fortune covering your grey hair," Geraldine quipped. "Is she going to open the nail bar? Might help keep her head above water, so to speak." Geraldine stood up and said, "Let's get you a top up. Stay there and put your feet up. Need a bigger footstool with your elephant feet!"

I waved my hand in the air to gesture, 'go away.' I am too tired to think of a suitable comical reply. Geraldine and me share even handed banter which on the surface sounds cruel but deep down we support each other through thick and thin.

Geraldine returned to the front room with two glasses of chilled prosecco and said, "I've put plates in the dishwasher. Usually charge extra but let you off this evening."

"Thank you so much," I said. "Save more wasps coming in. There were four in this morning."

Geraldine tutted. "Haven't you contacted the Pest Controller? The wasps will be inviting their family and friends for an all-night rave. They've got big families."

"I know, I know." I replied wearily. "Mum's asked Declan if can recommend a company. Must be someone in the pub who has had a wasp nest, and I don't mean as pets.!"

Geraldine grinned. "Your mum would love it if you had to move back with her. She may be using delaying tactics."

"I wouldn't put it past her, "I said. "Be lovely not to have to worry about washing and cooking but we would grate on each other's nerves and patience. No good pretending. Feel sorry for dad being the referee."

"You're mad missing out on cooking," Geraldine replied. "But you're around there enough so not missing out too much."

"Thankfully, you saved me from tonight's performance with Trevor and Angie. It's a farce."

Geraldine rolled her eyes. "Your mum must be fuming! What's the latest with Trevor and Miss Super Doll?"

"Don't ask," I sighed. "Feel sorry for Trevor. We can all see he's being taken for a ride but is still caught up in the honeymoon stage."

"I feel sorry for Angela, "Geraldine snapped. "Poor thing. She knows all the gossip and whispering. When's the last time you saw her?"

"She doesn't like people going to her house," I replied. "Isolation appears to be the best option, but she's built her own prison. Mum brings around shopping and cakes. She doesn't mind mum visiting. Mum's trying to persuade her to tidy the garden and encouraging her to take small steps. Her world is shattered. Mum's asked Angela for Sunday lunch on Bank Holiday weekend. You're welcome as always."

"I'm afraid I can't" Geraldine looked so disappointed. "It's sporting weekend with Seamus' friends. Kids really enjoy competing with the children, now they are getting older. I'll have to think of an excuse. Sunday roast at your home is like heaven. Not your home. We would have tea and toast and that would be pushing it."

I yawned and mumbled, "If I wasn't so tired, I would throw a cushion at you."

Geraldine could not resist the open goal and teased, "Oh poor Miss Overworked. Worn out? How did you get on with the meeting?"

"Don't ask, "I replied sharply. You don't want to know."

"Yes, I do," said Geraldine eagerly awaiting to hear the details. "Spill the beans."

I acquiesced. "Apart from Mrs Redbridge and Mrs Sharpe arguing about the colour of the door." Geraldine interjected, "what? You're joking?"

"Wish I was," I replied. "There'll be a frosty silence for three months. Awkward and more pressure for Wilberforce. Ivee dropped a cup and almost dropped the teapot on Humphrey. Finally, Councillor Carpenter arrived, and Doris told him not to sit on Ethel's chair!"

Geraldine gasped, "Ethel died five years ago? Vicar always says there is no such thing as ghosts! Aren't the PCC meetings supposed to be full of peace and patience. Sounds like a battlefield."

"Think a battlefield would be quieter and less stressful," I remarked. "All the rest is top secret."

"At least you had a day off today?" Geraldine enquired.

I turned my head. I cannot hide lies from her, so avoidance tactics seemed an option but proved to be a foolish choice.

"So, you didn't have a day off," said Geraldine. "What were you doing? Repairing the roof?"

"No, silly. Typing minutes. Wanted to help Naomi. She's in a right state."

Geraldine looked disapprovingly at me and said, "You'll be in an even worse state if you do anymore. Part time job – what's happened? Can't Naomi get someone else to help her? She has friends and family. Surely?"

I felt suitably reprimanded but continued to expand on my excuses, "she's still embarrassed or should I say humiliated. Doesn't want to face them."

"She'll have to," said Geraldine. Better for her to keep busy. Good distraction when someone has broken your heart and life apart. How selfish can you get? Men honestly. Must be someone out there not ruled by the content of their trousers! Glad I bumped into Seamus. Drives me mad but he won't be in the fast lane out. He knows where his bread is buttered and loves me and the kids to bits, thank God. Can't say the same for Morrigan: she's not going to change and I'm not bending to her complaints."

I observed the stress etched on Geraldine's face and said, "I thought she'd calm down now the children are older?"

"No, if anything she's worse," came the reply. "Her sharp tongue would slice metal. Seamus wants a quiet life – anything to shut her up. But she's not telling me which school the kids are going to."

Morrigan is Seamus' older sister, and she has inherited the disapproval and dislike of Geraldine from their mother.

I remain confused and distraught about the situation because it is draining for Geraldine and Seamus, but Morrigan is not going to tear down their resilience but is giving it a good try. She does not understand the strength of the love held by Geraldine and Seamus and cannot see past the niggles and banter. She wants them to argue. Maybe I am being too cynical but sense she wants them to separate. Geraldine and Seamus are weary from the heckling however the criticism is only strengthening their bond. The boys are growing tired of her interference and once Siobhan finds her feet, she will distance herself. Morrigan will be isolated from her family which is extremely sad but a result of her own making.

I asked, "she must be pleased they're going to Church?"

"Oh yeah," Geraldine replied. "As long as there's a shrine and statues of Mary. Please understand there is no disrespect to Mary. Seamus don't mind as long as they're going to church and go to a Church of England school. Other local schools are not suitable. Dread to think what is happening inside the gates."

I gave Geraldine a hug, "Can't understand how you cope. You're braver than me."

Geraldine replied, quick as a flash, "I know, and I can cook! Look at us sitting here like a pair of grannies. We'll have to get blankets and a cup of cocoa. No, I'm not giving up. There's still life in this girl. Right, we're going to hit the Town!"

"What now!?!" I shrieked.

Geraldine laughed loudly. "Don't be silly. You'd be asleep on the train. We're going to London. Disco! Do you remember 'Best Disco in Town.'?"

I grimaced. "Disco? Night Clubs now. They don't even dance. Jump up and down with mobiles in their hands. Squashed together like the underground. How can they chat anyone up?" Geraldine shook her head. "Good grief! We're like a pair of dinosaurs. It's online dating. No more, '*can I buy you a drink darling?*' Those were the days."

Flashbacks of grim scenes shimmied in my mind and replied, "and you used to say, '*Yeah, as long as you buy my mate one!*' Can clearly remember their expression. You always attracted the attention. I used to stand there like a right lemon."

"Gooseberry!" Geraldine giggled. "But prune is better description. It was your own fault. Told you to wear more fashionable clothes."

"You mean shorter skirts," I replied. "Mum would've gone mad! When you were otherwise occupied, I used to dance around - lots of space on the floor. Men didn't dance much. I was waiting for John Travolta. No chance of '*Night Fever*' in London."

Geraldine asked, "Do you remember those embarrassing slow dances? Makes me shudder to think about it. What were some of the chat-up lines, '*Do you come here often?*' or '*What's a nice girl doing in a place like this?*' YUK!"

I laughed out loud in recognition of those awkward moments but also felt a tinge of shame. I regret I cannot go back and change my words and actions. I looked at Geraldine and said, "how can I forget. Felt sorry for them. They didn't know where to put their hands and I used to hang round their necks."

Geraldine put her hands over her face, "when the lights went on, you could see what they really looked like!"

"Scary," I replied. "But not as scary as when I looked in the mirror. My cheap mascara and blue eye shadow smudged on my face. Must have taken ages for his mum to get the stains off his shirt."

"We used to try to get away quickly," Geraldine said. "But it was always you, saying, "just got to go to the loo," whilst I was wrestling with Casanova. "Oh, you're a good girl?" they used to say. I just wanted to leave."

"No, you didn't," I retorted. "I had to drag you from snogging around the corner. Followed by them saying, "I call you."

"Yeah, right!" Geraldine said sharply. All the false promises still stung. "Didn't hear from them. Those were the days! Anyway grannie, enough walking down memory lane or more like grubby alleyways, we're going out again."

"For one night only?" I replied.

"Yes, don't worry." Geraldine offered words of reassurance. "We'll be back before sun rise."

I started to feel anxious. "We'll have to book a hotel. I'm not coming home on the milk train."

"Milk train?" Geraldine laughed. "That's a blast from the past. Okay, we'll book a budget hotel. And we're sharing! Can't trust you with a single room – goodness knows who you'll bring back."

"Don't be stupid!" I retorted. "I wouldn't know what to do. And I am not having all those painful lady '*treatments*' just to get entangled with a drunk man. Anyway, I'd fall asleep before he took his shirt off."

"Don't be so grumpy." Geraldine replied. "Only teasing! We'll have hot chocolate and marshmallows in our room. Second thoughts! We'll have night caps."

Geraldine is gutsy and high-spirited. Always has been. We are a good balance. '*Ying and Yang*.' I trust her implicitly. Mum loves Geraldine and will always be grateful to her for continuing to look after me.

***

CHAPTER 6

A loud, "HELLO!" greeted me as I unlatched the gate of the rickety green picket fence. Pansies cascaded over the side of the hanging basket fixed on the wall by the Vicarage front door. The unkempt display reflected the un-groomed garden.

I like hanging baskets. Unfortunately, my one fell down last year. Dad keeps saying he will replace the wall fixture and mum promised to buy a selection of multi coloured pansies, fuchsia and 'creeping Jenny' for the grand opening ceremony but I would like a porch. I am not sure why? The vision is to have the space to sit down and take off shoes and leave umbrellas. It is not clear where all the visitors are coming from however the pseudo extension would be a nice stage entrance.

Hannah, dressed in a pastel pink and blue floral tea dress, called out, "please, come on in." Her welcome was as warm as the spring sunshine.

"Do you want me to take my shoes off?" I asked.

"Oh no!" Hannah replied. "All the carpets and floor tiles need to be replaced. The home improvements do not even make it on the first page of the '*To Do List*.' Would you like a cup of tea?

"Yes, please," I replied eagerly.

"How do you like your tea?" Hannah enquired.

"Strong! Like builder's tea."

Hannah laughed awkwardly. I paused before handing Hannah my contribution to the kitchen cupboard: a mixture of Fairtrade and Organic herbal teas, green tea, hot chocolate, and coffee. Also, the obligatory bag of sugar for new neighbours and a jar of honey from the hives in the local allotment.

Hannah looked quite overwhelmed and said, "You are so kind. Can I give you some money?"

"No, that's fine," I replied. "They are a belated moving in gift. The honey is scrummy. and the wasps who are using my house as an Air bnb, are in agreement.

"How awful!" Hannah gasped. "Hope the Pest Control company can help you soon?"

"My mum is on the case, so she'll have them there in no time." My lack of confidence in mum's fading enthusiasm for the issue seeped through the words and was acutely aware the tone of my voice changed.

Hannah deflated the bubble of worry by asking the magical question, "would you like a biscuit?"

"Yes, please! I shouldn't really. Had one too many mini eggs at Easter."

Hannah carried the tray into the front room and placed it on the small coffee table. I was hoping we could sit around the kitchen table, although was comforted by the threadbare carpet just in case I dropped my cup. The springs in the oversized aqua marine sofa were not as strong as anticipated therefore rapidly slid towards the back of the seat.

"I am sorry," Hannah's embarrassment etched over her face, and I wondered how many times she had to apologise the for state of disrepair of the church and the Vicarage. She continued, "we need to get extra cushions to put under the seats to help bolster them up."

"No problem, "I replied. "Just a bit concerned about getting out of the chair. My Pilates classes start next week. The leaflets show how I need to build a strong core. Strengthening my knee joints would be nice to start!"

"We could have classes in the church hall," Hannah's energetic idea was hit by reality. "One for the list of future events. The new roof is the priority. There is no benefit having a well-being class if everyone is soaking wet. Hillary is doing a great job filling in the gaps, but it is literally sticking plasters on a large wound."

I nodded in acknowledgement of the herculean task in front of this young family. "He's boarded up one of the windows in the hall. Does not look pretty but when needs must. Important to ensure there is no further damage to the leaded glazing and fragile frame. Unfortunately, these days, it is far too easy to rip out the old window completely rather than respecting and restoring the heritage."

"I entirely agree," said Hannah. "We need to repair and retain as much of the original fittings. However, when the rot has set in too deeply, we will have to install a new section. Appears the entire church roof needs replacing. Wil wants to keep the clock face and is trying everything possible to ensure it is not taken away."

"Absolutely, "I replied vigorously. "There would be a loud protest, in fact, an unusually boisterous action group if the clock is removed. Our lives have been run by that clock even when running fast or slow which has caused no end of problems especially at weddings!"

Hannah smiled and shook her head slowly in consideration of the heated disagreements about how many minutes late the bride turned up at the church. She asked, "on the topic of weddings please can I seek your advice about Kiyana?"

"Yes, sure, how can I help?"

"Thank you, "Hannah replied with relief folded into the mixture of matters in the bowl of ingredients constituting the role of a vicar's wife. "Not sure where to start." Hannah's voice trembled. "Kiyana is a beautiful singer."

I nodded firmly in agreement and said, "her voice sounds like silk. Difficult to find the words to give an adequate description."

Hannah continued hesitantly, "her fiancé, Tristan, is wonderful, so loving, but."

I interjected, "sadly, there is usually a but!"

Hannah put her left hand on her head indicating the level of stress. "Tristan's mother is furious about the engagement. She wants her only child to marry another consultant at the Neurology Hospital, or a successful barrister like his father. Her requirement is the same professional status."

I shook my head in sadness, "a profession of her choice no doubt. Not sure love or respect are top of the consideration for compatibility. Tristan's mother is Arabella?"

"Yes, "Hannah replied. "Mrs Anstruther-Gough-Calthorpe is extremely influential in the community and amongst the major donors towards St Laurence. I should not think about money in this set of circumstances at all, but wonder if there could be a compromise? I really don't want the church to collapse before we have a chance to serve the parish."

"I understand. If the building collapses the property developers will be queuing up to buy the land."

Hannah continued, "Wil says the bricks and mortar are only a rain shelter. We can pray on the village green if we have to."

I hesitated and was reluctant to make the following contribution however felt a need to continue, "oh, I agree in principle. I respectfully ask to consider; St Laurence is the heart of the community and a lifeline for the community. There is no intention to diminish the vocation of praise and worship. How incredibly sad to look around to see communities crumbling and we are living with the consequences. There is the old cliché, '*parents have children, but it takes a village to raise them.*' Especially poignant as more support services are closing and the reduction of shops results in the reduction of social interaction for some." I took a pause to think of a suitable suggestion. "There is always room for compromise. Unfortunately, Mrs Anstruther – Goff? Sorry, that's not right? What a surname; will there be enough space on the wedding certificate? Okay, I will start again; Arabella will not make any room to talk to me because she is a friend of Mrs Abbott, Jemima's mother. After the debacle on Easter Sunday, she is not going to help. Hopefully, Mrs Abbott will calm down in a few months.

Hannah's next question highlights her naivety, and lack of knowledge of the village politics in Old Botlean; which is entirely understandable. "Should I talk to Tristan's father?"

"Sounds a good idea," I replied in an upbeat manner before explaining the backdrop of the scenery. "I'm afraid, there is another, but; how can such a small word lead to such pitfalls? Although Albert is a first-class Barrister, his authority in the court room does not stand any ground at home. Arabella rules the roost. I can ask my dad to speak to him; I think Albert goes to the same golf club."

"If they push Tristan too far, he will elope with Kiyana." Hannah's words contained as much worry as shown on her taught face. "They'll return to her family in Jamaica."

My contribution echoed the sadness which should be one of the happiest times in their lives. "Kiyana left her home to live near her fiancé. That is a big sacrifice, only to be confronted with Arabella."

Hannah nodded despondently. "We are overjoyed Kiyana is here to lead the children's choir. They love her. I am being selfish – her happiness and mental health are the important factor. Mrs Anstruther-Gough-Calthorpe, I mean, Arabella, is not the best pleased because Tristan has chosen to be a Christian out of respect for Kiyana and her family but has also opened his eyes to the big questions in life and how much he needs God. His mother thinks her large estate will save them."

"Don't blame them in one sense," I replied. "However, when we are feeling brave, we can pose the question, 'who sets the moral compass?' Food for thought although Arabella may chew it up and spit it out, so to speak." I continued with the dreadful image of Arabella lingering in my mind. "We could play the wild card. Oops, sorry. Not the best analogy. I shouldn't listen to Seamus and most certainly should not paraphrase his jokes."

Hannah looked confused, "Seamus?"

I offered an apology and explained, "Geraldine O'Connor's husband."

"Ah yes!" Geraldine's daughter, Siobhan, goes to the same school as Rebecca and Sarah. Siobhan has inherited her father's sense of humour minus the colourful words thankfully.

"How are Rebecca and Sarah settling in? "I asked. "New home, new school, and new neighbours. Big move in a short period of time and in so many different ways."

Hannah remained relaxed and was not perturbed by the thought of the size of the mountain they have to climb. "They're fine, thank God. More resilient than their parents. Although a struggle to get them to tidy their bedroom. Otherwise, they are a blessing. Once they find their feet, I'm sure they will get involved with the events in the church hall. One day at a time."

"Wise words!" I affirmed Hannah's clear distinction between encouragement and enforcement to assist supporting the church. "Excuse me, I am disrupting the flow of the conversation. My reference to '*wild card*' was a clumsy attempt to suggest an unexpected character. Jovial and eccentric. Helps to lower the guard. Humphrey? He coped really well with Mrs Redbridge in the PCC meeting."

Hannah smiled lightly. "Yes, Doris can get quite animated, but she has a wealth of knowledge which is valued. It is certainly worth asking Humphrey. He is an amiable character and can enquire if Arabella would like to organise a fund-raising event in her home? If she accepts the suggestion, we may receive an invitation."

I interrupted, "almost certain she'll agree and the whole parish will be invited. A large social event is her *raison d'être*. Oh my, showing my age, do you remember the TV programme The Good Life?"

Hannah looked upwards to the memory space we all so often refer to. She paused for thought. "Uhmm. Yes, I think so? Was Geraldine the goat in the show?"

I laughed loudly and recorded the comment in my mind's cassette tape, only to be replayed to Geraldine when I phone her this evening. "That's the one. Arabella would overshadow the character, Margo. Putting that to one side for a moment, Arabella will manage a grand event for the community and ideal opportunity to raise funds. Her friends will offer generous support out of fear of being outclassed by their acquaintances. You never know, there may be a new church roof sooner than expected."

Hannah appeared troubled. "I feel bad. Are we exploiting the situation? Sounds quite devious?"

I set out my case for the defence, "I don't think it is exploiting the situation: raising funds for repairs will require creative thinking. The event will be another chance for you and Wilberforce to meet more people in the community."

"Whilst you're here," Hannah said expectantly. "Can I ask you about Bernadette? She really is worrying me. "Sorry, do you have time?"

"Yes. Happy to help. Will take a couple of days to discuss all the concerns about Bernadette. I am only joking."

Hannah asked a question which was music to my ears. "Can I get you another cup of tea?"

"Yes, please." I replied enthusiastically and pulled myself up from the sofa with a lot of huffing and puffing. "Let me help you. I'll bring the plate and the crumbs with me."

Hannah placed the old-fashioned kettle on the stove. Memories flooded my mind of mum busily baking and making tea in tune to the high-pitched whistle of the kettle proclaiming boiling point. The non-matching mugs depict scenery of holidays of yesteryear: Rome and Wittenberg, in Germany.

"Bernadette is heartbroken, "Hannah said. "She was inconsolable when I last saw her; is there anything I can, or should do?"

"An instant husband would be the answer to her prayers and desire." I replied flippantly. "Sorry. I am being facetious. Do not mean to be disrespectful to you. Geraldine and me have known Bernadette since we worked in the City of London. What has happened to the time? The clock is definitely running fast! A simple summary is – Bernadette does not like being a spinster, to put it mildly. Sometimes her pent-up frustration bursts out and I'm afraid you met her on one of her dark days."

"She says she does not want to return to the church services and wants to be on her own."

I acknowledged Hannah's description of the encounter and looked at her knowingly. "Being a Lone Ranger is not going to her help her. She might go to the Christianity Explored course especially if the invitation is delivered by you. I want to continue to be her friend, but the monologues are increasing in length and intensity. Mum has asked her to Sunday lunch on 5th May – the bank holiday weekend. I'll have a chat to her then. Mum doesn't tolerate her long speeches nor her pity parties. Mum does not approve of her close friendship, I am trying to be polite, with George."

"Ah! Does he live in Old Botlean?" Hannah asked naively.

"No!" I replied emphatically. "He lives with his wife! I'll stop there because it's not fair. She is not here to defend herself or provide a plausible explanation. Bernadette cries incessantly when there is an upcoming wedding, and the baptism will trigger a meltdown."

Hannah gave me a quizzical look. "Baptism?"

"Rachael Reardon would like to arrange the baptism of her twins. I left a message for Wilberforce."

"Sorry," Hannah's apologetic tone was another insight into the enormity of the task in front of her. "I'll remind him. What would we do without you?"

"You've got an awful lot on your plate," I said reassuringly. "Rachael is not in a hurry: handsome boys but what a handful. Her husband, Shaun, is stressed worrying about money and the lack of sleep does not help. Rachael wants to return to work to contribute towards the household bills, but the cost of childminding will counteract any additional income. Also, she will miss precious moments with her children which maybe an old-fashioned view."

Hannah sighed. "I really would like to get around to meet and support as many of the Christian family as possible. We hope to set up a mother and baby club."

I placed my hand gently on Hannah's arm. "You have made a tremendous start. Your support is much appreciated and much needed. Reverend Wiggett did as much as practical. A segment of the congregation felt more at ease because he was not married however there are only so many hours in the day for one person to work."

"Oh, that reminds me," said Hannah. "I need to finalise the care rota for James. Molly cannot cope looking after him and volunteering at the church. I know she will not give in willingly. We do not want to make her ill."

"Mum can make enquiries. The local Councillor, Timothy, will know who to contact."

"Thank you," Hannah replied. "His cottage is in fairly good condition: most importantly the water and the heating are working. The interior design needs renewing. Not sure James would approve of the phrase, modernising."

I laughed in recognition of the amusing observation and said, "Declan knows a lot of workmen. One might be able to volunteer with the DIY."

"I'm afraid a volunteer is all we can afford. The budget is at full stretch. We do believe in miracles so there will be adequate provision in God's timing. The waiting in the middle is the tricky part – the real test of faith."

I picked up my bag in readiness to leave and missed mum's check out routine but would not admit that to her face "Thank you for the tea and biscuits. Please try to have a rest. If you need any help, please ask."

Hannah's request was delivered swiftly. "Would you be able to help with the community lunch on Friday 17th May? We had to move the lunch from the usual Tuesday and know there will be mutterings about the change however we have to shuffle commitments around the two bank holidays in May."

"Yes, that'll be okay. Molly and me can do battle, once again, in the kitchen over who does the washing up and who does the drying up. Mum is baking delicious delights for the community pantry which needs a new security lock." Hannah giggled revealing a glimpse of her youthful nature before returning to carrying the weight of expectation and examination by the parish."

***

CHAPTER 7

"Dance classes start next week!" Dad roared with laughter. He never misses the chance to tease me, which is fun most of the time, but not when laden down with heavy bags and tripping over the loose step at the entrance of the church hall.

"Thanks Dad!" My mockery flew over dad's head therefore I continued on the quest for assistance. "Instead of laughing at me you can help me with these bags."

"What on earth have you got there?" dad asked.

"Another supply of mum's homemade cakes and shortbread biscuits. My mission is to lock them in the pantry. She does not want '*Uncle Tom Cobley and all*' getting their hands on them before Sunday. You would need an iron bar to get through the layers of Sellotape on the tins."

"Please let me help, "said Mervyn Hopkins who appeared to be losing weight rapidly. He now uses a walking stick because his steps are faltering, however, he soldiers on hoping no one will notice the decline in his health. Kiyana heard him mumble, "widower without a purpose" when asked the notorious question, "and what do you do for a living?" Mum will know what to do for the best and we can look into the social housing options. Giving up his home will almost be as traumatic as saying the final farewell to his darling Gwen at the graveside last year.

I smiled at Mervyn and said jokingly, "You are kind, thank you. Not like my lazy dad!"

Mervyn seemed startled at the perceived direct attack at my dad. Our exchange of banter can be quite sharp and difficult for others to comprehend. Mervyn's flat cloth cap stayed securely in place as he carried the bags to the kitchen.

"Cheeky!" Dad called out. "Look, I'm putting the chairs back. Logan gives you the keys for one afternoon and you release the Kraken!"

"Dad! What are you going on about? Did you smuggle in a hip flask of whiskey?"

Basil Bloome, member of the Parochial Church Council, came to the rescue to clear the confusion. "The film, Clash of the Titans: the Kraken is a legendary sea monster."

"Thank you, Basil," I replied. "Now I understand. Dad does talk gibberish sometimes and am sure he does not think I look like a sea monster? Anyway, did you enjoy the chess club?"

"Very much," Basil said enthusiastically." Your dad is wonderful at explaining the game and all the different pieces."

"Sounds good but he is still on probation." Out of the corner of my eye I saw dad smirking but did not let his reaction put me off track. "Not sure if he will get the final seal of approval to the Chess Master of St Laurence. The vicar is mulling over the options for the Man Cave Club. Although I think a cave will be warmer than in here. Where is that draught coming from?"

"It's chess not draughts!" Dad sniggered.

"Stop it!" I said forcefully. "Told you no more karaoke and no more dad jokes!"

Dad gave me a hug and said, "I know, but they make you smile which is nice to see."

His words are few however each letter represents a heartbeat. He would love to say a lot more if he could find the definition in his mind's dictionary. Just three letters of the alphabet – dad - conjures up emotions far deeper than I can comprehend. No words are adequate to describe my gratitude for being blessed with a dad who has boundless energy, empathy, and endurance.

"Hello! I didn't see you there. How are you?" I asked.

"Not too bad," Hamish MacDougall replied wearily. Hamish, is a confirmed bachelor, retired and lives in sheltered accommodation. His family's roots, sadly fractured over five years ago, are in Argyll. The church family offer him a detour from the isolation however Hamish unashamedly pronounces he enjoys his own company. A certain level of social interaction is healthy therefore was delighted to see him at the Man Cave Club. When I saw Hamish talking to Mervyn, I hoped my clumsy attempt at matchmaking would be fruitful. Hamish told Molly, not always the best option, a couple of the rooms in his block of flats are being refurbished. Discretion is not one of Molly's strengths: she did not waste any time sharing the breaking news with the congregation. Her tactics drive some to distraction, however in this set of circumstances, the gossip led to a possibility that no one could have imagined. I can assist Mervyn with the paperwork, and Wilberforce will support the application in conjunction with a character reference from Reverend Wiggett.

Hopefully, our prayers will be answered, and the outcome will combat the loneliness felt so strongly by Mervyn.

I walked towards Mervyn to say goodbye and thank him for coming to support the MCC [Man Cave Club] "Would you like to come to lunch on Sunday? Don't worry, it's at my mum's home. She is the Chef Master. I keep to kitchen cleaning duties – far safer for the guests. Basil will be there."

Mervyn, overwhelmed by the invitation and my elongated explanation, replied reservedly. "Thank you. I hope to have a quiet weekend. There should be a few extra programmes on the television as it is a bank holiday. I may go to The Old Door Inn on Sunday to meet Hamish and his friends from the care home. I think they are allowed out each week."

Mervyn's words conjured up a mixture of joy and apprehension in equal measure. I did not attempt to correct the commentary: a popular perception of sheltered accommodation This was not the time or place to educate and encourage Mervyn to explore the benefits of independent living within a support framework which will step in when required. Privacy is respected. Once Mervyn gets chatting with Hamish's friends, I am sure the misunderstanding will be banished although the fear of, 'giving in and giving up', will cling on for a while. "Well, have a nice time. If you change your mind about Sunday, call the office."

I struggled with the hinges on the unpainted door to ensure the bolts closed properly. Logan would shout from the roof top if I left the door unlocked. However, he will have to wait until the church roof is repaired. Ironically, a thief could take down the temporary board on the window before you could say, "why is it so cold in here?"

Dad looked at me in disbelief and said, "you're brave or just forgetful. Mum will go through the roof, another dad joke to keep you entertained."

"Please get to the point if there is one?" I was exasperated with the riddle.

"You really are going to risk spoiling your mother's table plan on Sunday; boy, girl, boy girl etc...? If Mervyn is a last-minute guest, we will have to invite someone else?"

"Dad, please do not exaggerate. Will be okay. I can ask Molly to join us."

"Now you've gone into a parallel universe!" Dad said with an ever-growing tense tone which was not like him. "Can you see mum and Molly in the same kitchen, especially mum's kitchen. 'Fools rush in where angels fear to tread!'"

"Stop it!" I nudged dad's arm. "Talking of fools, if Trevor had retained one ounce of sense he would be there with Angela, and that would help balance the numbers. He better not dare come anywhere near our home on Sunday. Not that he knows there is a special lunch?"

Dad's face wrinkled in angst. "I may have mentioned it. Trevor's not that insensitive, he's probably going on holiday."

I gasped, "Dad! How can you be so naïve? He would stay away but he's new wife leads him by the collar. Let's hope she is having a long Spa break or mum will be throwing something organic in her direction!"

"It'll be alright on the night, and day!" Dad said with a cheeky, reassuring grin on his face.

"Love you!" I said before asking the vital question, "how many more sleeps until roast day?"

***

CHAPTER 8

"SERVIETTES! SERVIETTES!" Mum screeched at the top of her voice.

"Okay, okay," I acknowledged the order. "I'll go upstairs to get them."

"Make sure you don't crease them. I ironed and starched them yesterday."

I mouthed, "Starch?" Dad looked at me intently and put his fingers to his lips. "Ssshh! Be quiet!" He whispered. "We are walking on eggshells. Another dad joke."

"William. I can hear you!" Mum's formality raised the red flag warning of a pending explosion of frustration. "Can you come and take the rubbish out and put the peelings in the recycling bin."

"On my way." Dad had a cheeky grin on his face before he asked an uncharacteristic bold question. "Do you want me to get another bottle of wine? Declan has just had a nice vintage delivered."

"I need you here!" Mum squealed. "I don't care what vintage or bottle he has. I know you; you'll be in The Old Door Inn having a few aperitifs and then just by chance will be watching the sport and won't be rushing back."

The sky blue and white colour scheme for the table setting was as cool as a cucumber unlike mum who was at boiling point. She excels in cooking and is usually okay. Only huffs and puffs if one of her legendary roast potatoes falls on the floor. But, when there are guests with such an eclectic mixture of characters, her nerves are stretched, and her high-pitched voice is operatic. Of course, dad makes matters worse. Not the time nor the place for dad jokes. Overall, he knows the boundary walls and beams with pride inside about how his wife manages every minute detail of a dinner party.

"Do you want me to make the gravy?" I asked.

"NO!" Mum's sharp reply cut though the steam in the kitchen. "Sorry, Blodwyn. Not today. Can you check all the glasses are clean and open the new handwash containers in the bathroom and check the towels are clean? Your father may have dishevelled them."

The first guest to arrive was Angela Teacher. She looked nervous. "Lovely to see you," I said softly. "Please, let me take your jacket?" Before Angela could reply, mum bounded down the hall and bellowed, "ANGELA! So glad you could come." I thought, "*the poor woman; the first outing to a social event for a long time and she is nearly bowled over by mum.*"

"Would you like a drink?" Mum was exhilarated by the presence of her good friend and how many hurdles Angela had cleared to get here. "Ruth will get you one, won't you Blodwyn?" I looked at Angela and smiled smoothly. "Yes, mum still calls me Blodwyn." Angela reciprocated – nodded in response to the light-hearted comment and her shoulders relaxed.

Bernadette Bunting was the last guest to arrive. Her opening line was, "so glad you opened the door. Is my lipstick smudged?"

"No!" I replied with a tinge of impatience mixed with irritation which I struggled to hide. "Glad you could make it. Best go in, we're slightly late for Mum's timetable. Believe me – not a wise move."

Bernadette's reply was not apologetic in fact the complete opposite. "Gladys will make an exception for me. Have the flowers arrived? I ordered them yesterday – the long stem white roses – your mum's favourite?" Bernadette teetered into the dining room wearing classic Christian Louboutin spectacular glossy black patent pumps. Her matte lipstick matched the signature red sole. The ivory-coloured tailored belted pencil dress seemed inappropriate for a Sunday roast, but Bernadette's fashion style is representative of her personality. The Louis Vuitton mini bag fitted snugly under the designated chair between Thomas Carpenter, the local Councillor, and Lester Plum, the Postmaster.

The wine flowed and the sound of the voices rose to a crescendo – Bernadette being the principal conductor. Humphrey Crook, a Church Warden, complimented mum on the spectacular Sunday roast (his words not mine) and delicate floral table decorations. "Not taken from Basil's Garden, I hope," Bernadette cast her loaded hook hoping someone would take the bait. She continued with her diatribe, "you know? The ones Ivee snatched. Think Wilberforce made an error employing such an inexperienced member of staff." I interjected forcefully, "Ivee is doing a wonderful job. Will take a while to learn all the aspects of a Children and Family Minister. There is a lot to learn. You need to be patient with new staff." Bernadette pouted and returned to her glass of wine.

"Yes, you do need a lot of patience with new staff and usually reaps rewards," said Christine Panayiotou, the owner of the hairdressing shop in Old Botlean. "Although I could not keep one trainee on because otherwise, I would have ended up in a lawsuit. Orange hair is not a popular look." Christine's contribution cooled the heated exchange between Bernadette and me.

"I applaud you for keeping your business opened." The recognition and praise came from Timothy Carpenter. "Unfortunately, an increasing number cannot withstand the financial pressure. Villages such as Old Botlean and the High Street are vital for the community."

Bernadette jumped in quickly, "I entirely agree. You are so thoughtful." Her eyes widened and her eyelashes fluttered like a butterfly in a hurry. Mum's intuition kicked in instantly and turned towards Timothy. "How is your wife?" "Thank you for asking," he replied. "Her mother came out of hospital on Friday. Margaret will stay with her for a couple of weeks. All sounded okay this morning when she called." Dad diverted the conversation using a strategic move akin to the skill he applies during a game of chess. "Are you enjoying your new role, John?" The Treasurer at St Laurence, John Eton, replied hesitantly but with professional clarity. "Very well, thank you. Wilberforce and Hannah are a strong couple and will be a significant support for the community once they settle in. Wilberforce is determined to ensure there is more transparency in the accounting records. When the website is up and running there will be a page dedicated to the income and outgoings. The notes Ruth typed after the last Parochial Church Council are helpful."

"Yes. She enjoyed the PCC meeting didn't you sweetheart?"

I tuned into dad's mischievous undertone and waited in trepidation for the punch line.

"Ruth told me all the details." He could barely hold in his laughter.

"I did not!" My retaliation was swift. "I can assure you, John, no confidential information was shared with my adorable and annoying father. He has an incredible imagination but is not blessed with the talent to tell jokes that are actually funny."

"Bit harsh." Bernadette chipped in with a sharp-edged sword i.e. her tongue.

Dad laughed, "not at all. I love my daughter; however, I love to wind her up even more."

I scowled. Dad added quickly. "Only sometimes." Dad stood up and kissed me on the cheek and squeezed my arm to comfort me and publicly show our close bond. Bernadette is envious of how close I am to mum and dad. Maybe, I am being unfair, but it is true. Her father left the family home when she was two and there has been no contact since. Her mother now lives in the south of France with her latest fiancé. She insisted they get engaged before living together which was a conundrum initially however discovered she has a jewellery box filled with diamond rings.

Angela sat quietly in the corner next to mum and Humphrey who was her male partner in the sense of the table plan.

"Oh Angela," said Lester. "I meant to say, the new set of stamps have arrived. Would you like me to save the special first day cover?"

"Thank you. Yes." Angela's voice was barely audible however we all smiled politely. The next statement surprised us, not only in volume but content. "I can come into the Post Office tomorrow if that is, okay?"

"I look forward to seeing you," Lester replied gleefully.

"Are you managing to get more stock?" Timothy asked.

"It's getting better." Lester replied and sighed with relief. "Do not know how we are going to keep up with the online deliveries and encourage people to post letters and cards when there are e-cards, e-mails and all sorts of weird and wonderful technology."

"Stronger community will help rebuild and build local business." Timothy replied. "We must spend time with the owners and spend money in the shops. The Post Office is an integral financial centre, especially as bank branches are closing. I sense we will lose vast numbers in the next few years."

"I am worried about access to banks," said Christine. "I want customers to continue to have the option to use cash, I do not want to push customers away. We are struggling as it is. Luxuries and hairdressing are top of the list to cut from household budgets. The nail bar will be opening next week. So, we need your prayers. Ruth, you are one of the first bookings."

"Can't wait," I replied with delight. "Will have the Swarovski crystals on the little fingers as a treat. Geraldine thinks I'm crazy, but we haven't been out for a long time."

"A night on the town. Sounds fantastic." Bernadette's excitement seemed excessive until the penny dropped. She thinks she is invited. How on earth am I going to explain the 'girls' night out' is just Geraldine and me. Mum observed Bernadette's hyperactive body language and exuberance and stopped her in her tracks before the monologue started about the arrangements, the outfits, and the morning after. "I need help with the coffee." Mum directed her gaze towards Bernadette. "Would appreciate your help in the kitchen."

"Yes. Oh, yes, of course." Bernadette's flustered response highlighted her exasperation at not being able to continue. "Ooh, I do like Nespresso. You know, George Clooney? How suave and sophisticated. Where is your machine?" Bernadette's enquiry was met with an introduction to a different topic. Mum entered the realm of reality. "Bernadette, you are a beautiful woman. You know that and everyone else knows that. I empathise and recognise the loneliness. You try to hide it, but I can see through the act. I will support you as much as practical. But and this is a BIG but. Ruth needs to heal at her own pace amongst those who will encourage her not drain her. This is a blunt request. Please keep your distance from my daughter, for now at least. Geraldine is her closest friend, and she needs to spend time with her, that is, going out next week. We are not wrapping Ruth in cotton wool. Geraldine most certainly will not – quite the opposite. Tough love is her approach with an insight how much she treasures her friendship."

Bernadette looked stunned. Not knowing how to react to such firm but fair comments. "Of course, yes," she said reluctantly not wanting to admit the truth. "Fully understand.

Hannah comes to my home which is nice. Quite different from Rev. Wiggett." They both laughed which softened the straight lines of the conversation.

I heard the purring of the Jaguar engine as the vehicle approached the drive and I gulped in anticipation of the upcoming confrontation.

"Humphrey, please show Angela the new rockery in the garden. The Heavenly Blue shrub you gave me is stretching out beautifully and compliments the surrounding border."

"I would love to," Humphrey replied enthusiastically. "Now, what is the Latin name? Lithodora diffusa? I am sure it is. I digress. Your prowess as a gardener almost matches your culinary skills however the chef's hat is taller."

The tap on the front door was light but persistent. I gestured for mum to come into the hall and said, "they won't go away." Mum's face turned to stone and spat out, "leave this to me!"

"I just popped around to give William his prize for winning the golf tournament last week." Trevor nervously held up a bottle of the finest Whiskey in a custom engraved wooden presentation box.

"Well. You can just pop away." Mum spoke quietly, but the ferocity was unmistakable. "You go now. Not in a few minutes. Now! I thought you were stupid to throw away a decent marriage but can clearly see how truly selfish you are – beyond words."

"We only wanted to give Willian the gift." Angie, Trevor's wife piped up and proffered an excuse covered in treacle – sweet but sticks in your mouth.

"I am not gullible and stupid enough to believe your lies like your husband. Or should I say, husband for now, until you get bored." Mum's vitriol was vicious and was like watching a pressure cooker exploding. "You know Angela is here. William told Trevor during the week. Showing your true colours. GOOD! Hopefully will open a few eyes. Take one last look at our home because you will not be invited again."

Angie pouted like a spoilt child, but the edge of her mouth showed a glimmer of a grin. She thrived on stirring up trouble. I cannot understand why she continues to torment Angela. Does she feel threatened? Or, just fearful of losing her 'meal ticket' before meeting a younger and richer man who matches her vision of an idyllic handsome prince.

***

CHAPTER 9

"WHAT? CAN'T HEAR YOU!" Geraldine shouted as we stood by the crowded bar in a crowded venue. "COCKTAIL. PLEASE." My voice crackled under the strain of bellowing a reply. Once Geraldine was told the price, she mouthed, "only one."

"Between us?" Confusion crumpled my face as I struggled to be heard. Geraldine nodded and pointed to a table in the corner.

"Are you sure we used to come here?" I asked.

"Yes. You must remember dancing around until the early hours."

I racked my brain, '*was this really the venue for our monthly girl's night out?*' I looked around in disbelief and replied in bewilderment. "There is not enough space to move never mind dance. How could you perform Night Fever in the middle of this mayhem?"

Geraldine laughed and nudged my arm as a young trendy man swaggered towards our table. We both puffed ourselves up which looked as ridiculous as it sounds.

"Good evening, ladies." He charmed us with his deep brown eyes and smooth, shiny, long black hair.

"Good evening." We replied in harmony. Geraldine mumbled. "it's a very, very, good evening." I giggled and whispered, "stop it! You're a married woman."

His voice was as smooth as his olive skin. "So, ladies, are you having a nice time?"

I thought, '*how polite*.' My naivety was shattered by the next question.

"Are you here for a bet?"

"PARDON?" Geraldine shrilled.

His enquiry was malicious and malevolent but was delivered with a smile that would melt an ice sculpture and I mean of prize-winning dimension.

"You are rather mature. My mates thought you came in to win a bet. Or a game of truth or dare?"

I saw steam coming out of Geraldine's ears, metaphorically speaking. She took a deep breath before delivering the knockout blow. "Well, mister! The truth is you and your mates are rather immature and wouldn't win a bet even if there was only one horse in the race."

***

"My shoe is stuck," I cried.

"Stuck to what?" Gerladine replied impatiently.

"My foot!"

The delicious aroma of the takeaway pizza, we smuggled into our hotel room, filled the air. My appetite increased after dancing on a small square in a pub near Charing Cross station – a short walk from Covent Garden – our old stomping ground.

"Wasn't like this in our day," I murmured.

"No, "said Geraldine indignantly. "We didn't have to pay for a hotel room. We danced until dawn and got a taxi. Not giving up at 11 p.m.!"

"Not giving up," I moaned in agony. "Just a pause."

"Pause for what?" Geraldine snapped. "Unless you are going back out in your slippers or risking bare feet, you're not capable of going anywhere besides the bathroom."

"Oh, stop it! You're just like dad. Never mind my feet. Just want pizza."

Geraldine agreed with the craving for our late supper. We tucked into the delightful tomato and mozzarella slices topped with basil leaves.

"Would madam like tea?" My impression of a butler was lacking authenticity.

"No." Geraldine replied sharply. "Madam would like a glass of prosecco from the bottle I tucked into my small case."

I sat up on the single bed and stretched out my legs. The throbbing in my feet eased and I reflected, "Seems like another world, when we worked in The City. Do you miss it?"

"No way." Geraldine's emphatic reply was followed by her recollection of our time together in London. "Can't believe we lived amongst such noise, but anything was better than being squeezed in the tin of sardines with all the other poor commuters."

We shared a studio flat, near Farringdon tube station: rented from a work colleague who was on an international assignment in Australia. He preferred the property occupied to alleviate the risk of squatters. Walking to work was a blessing however the management took advantage of our proximity by using coercive comments such as - "You don't mind staying later – only a hop, skip and a jump for you, young ladies, unlike poor Anastasia travelling two hours a day. I rubbed my eyes and recalled, "we were too tired to hear the noise. How did we manage to work such long hours and not collapse?"

"Never mind the work," Geraldine laughed. "How did we manage to wash and dry our clothes in a studio the size of my bedroom. I really looked forward to you going away to client events."

"Thank you very much. Love you too."

Geraldine's face mellowed and in a calmer tone she asked, "did Sean keep in contact?"

"No." My face tipped towards the wall, but I could not hide my emotions. She sees through me like a clear glass window and has always had this intuition. Not intrusive but in an inordinate level of loving care.

"Everyone was jealous." Geraldine nudged my arm. "He was good looking, which is the understatement of the year."

"Sure was; and he knew it. They are the worst. The thrill of the hunt and then they get bored and move on to the next prey."

"Bit over dramatic," Geraldine chuckled. "At least your liaison was in a four-star hotel in York and not in our studio."

"York, and Kendal." I confessed.

"KENDAL!?!" Geraldine squealed.

"Keep your voice down." I waved my hand in front of Geraldine's face. "We'll get thrown out for anti-social behaviour.

"Never mind my voice; time to break open the crisps and listen to a fascinating bedtime story."

"Once upon a time," I whispered.

"Okay. Okay. Clever clogs. Just spill the beans."

This was the one secret I kept from Geraldine.

***

I met Sean during a work event over a period of five days in York. The location was near The Shambles, a picturesque historic street. Pressurised preparations for power-point presentations led to drinks in the evenings to alleviate the stress. Sean was a representative from a key Client therefore a lot of focus was directed towards him. On the surface a charming man; cool, sophisticated, and a smooth operator. Underneath, a vulnerability that made him more alluring. To this day I do not know if the vulnerability was part of the act, however, in rare, relaxed moments he let his guard down and I glimpsed into intense sadness. The other candidates and work colleagues were indeed envious, and I admit, I thrived on the reaction as I danced on a metaphorical cloud – infatuated and intrigued with his complex character. My director, although against relationships between work colleagues, did not bat an eyelid. In a cynical moment, I think he encouraged the liaison, to endorse the bonus for Sean which sounds sordid now, but amidst the entrapment of the Corporate Machine it all felt completely normal.

Sean took me on personal tours of York. I thrived on the attention and affirmation of my professional skills and appearance. My director was delighted, and he approved the day off on Friday and paid for the Executive Suite for the weekend: a benefit in kind to reward my excellent performance. (His words not mine.)

Deep down I knew Sean was not a stayer but kept hold of the dream. Sean hired a cottage in the picturesque town of

Kendal. We enjoyed visiting historical buildings and walking in the glorious countryside. Sean hired a car so we could go to The World of Beatrix Potter in the centre of Bowness-on-Windermere. It is fair to say it was not in his top ten of attractions, but he humoured me; no doubt motivated by enhancing the professional relationship with my director.

I am not sure why I kept the trip a secret. I suppose I did not want Geraldine to talk me out of it so I made up a stupid excuse or should I say told a bear faced lie: a wife of a client invited me to stay in her cottage. Geraldine was over the moon to have the studio to herself and maybe a casual boyfriend. She did not take much notice which is most unlike her. In reality I think she knew and understood Sean and me only had a short span of time so it was best to get the moment out of our system.

***

"Bernadette was spitting frogs." Geraldine giggled.

"Why?" My enquiry was made from under the duvet as I snuggled in my cool cotton butterfly print pyjama set.

"Well," said Geraldine, "she had the pick of the bunch, and she did a lot of harvesting."

"Miaow." I tried to purr but my yawn overtook the attempt at humour.

"Don't play Miss Innocent. You thought the same." Geraldine retorted. "But Bernadette wanted what she couldn't have, still does."

"What happened to Mr Andover?" My eye lids became heavier with each breath.

"Who? Ah yes, George. He went back to his wife: he wasn't happy but wanted to try an affair to boost his ego. Same old story."

Geraldine's persistent request for me to brush my teeth did not disturb my deep sleep.

***

"Oh, why do I have such stinky breath?" My sore throat crackled.

"I tried to get you to brush your teeth. You wouldn't listen and couldn't get you to wake up. Snoring like an old ship's horn. Thankfully, there's not many people on the train. They'll have to wear gas masks!"

"Stop it," I said whilst trying to keep two fresh mints in my mouth. "At least I'm not carrying an empty bottle of wine with me."

"Excuse me." Geraldine replied with the strict sound of a headmistress. "It's an empty bottle of Prosecco. The finest vintage."

"It still smells." I giggled.

"You're getting grumpier by the day," Geraldine teased. "Old granny better go home to bed."

"I wish," I groaned. "Promised Hannah I'd volunteer at the Community Lunch."

Geraldine rebuked me. "Don't be silly, you can hardly keep your eyes open. You'll scare the guests with mascara still stuck to your face and hair like a scare crow. They've got plenty of volunteers. Ruth. You can't save the world."

"I know. I know. But I promised and feel so sorry for Hannah." I foolishly put forward an invitation which I knew would be declined due to crucial commitments. "You could come and hold my hand or prop me up?"

"No way! I have to face the fallout from Daddy Day care and overnight oversight. I dread to think what I'll find. Seamus will be in panic mode by now because he knows the clock is ticking. Dear God, please help me keep my mouth shut - just for the first five minutes at least. If he meets me with a bunch of flowers, we are in real trouble. Prefer him to just grunt at me from the laptop - confirmation all is sort of okay."

***

"Look at yer!" Molly called out, even louder than usual. "You look worse than I feel and that's saying something. Have you been dragged backwards through a hedge? Go home before you collapse. We've got enough to do beside carrying you home."

"But I promised Hannah I'd help." I said feebly.

Molly looked at me and tutted. "You're no good to man or mouse in your state. Get some sleep because it looks like you didn't get any last night."

I thanked Molly but am not comfortable being in her debt. I now owe her a favour in return. An elephant would be proud of the length and depth of her memory. She remembers every stitch and every dropped stitch. Such a burden - to carry so many memories on your back and have them engraved in your heart. Aches and pains that can hinder our ability to enjoy the beauty surrounding us and exclude us from the relationships searching for us.

***

CHAPTER 10

Molly scuttled into the kitchen holding a tray full of empty cups and said, "you don't need to be doing the washing up. I'll be alright. Know more about it than anyone here, that's for sure."

"I do need to wash up. Believe me, I really do." My words spluttered out as I threw the Tupperware container into the sink with such a force the water hit me in the face.

"You'll need a flannel to dry yourself," said Molly. "Should've had a wash this morning in your bathroom. Far more space in there."

"Sorry." I tried to sound suitably apologetic but was just about to blow a gasket (metaphorically speaking.) "If I hear one more word about the colour of the that door my language will be far more colourful."

Molly offered the age-old-solution to ease my stress, "Would you like a cup of tea?"

"Yes please. An extra strong one."

The water poured over the side of the sink. "Oooo, I am going to scream in a minute!" My exasperation was met by a calm and youthful voice. "Please do not scream. Sunshine brings a smile."

"Yes. Yes," I said impatiently. "I'll smile in a minute when I can unblock the sink."

"We used to have the same problem in the student kitchen; lots and lots. I will not repeat what we found in the pipes. Bad smell? I do not know the strong word in English."

The familiar accent and understated soothing voice encircling the atmosphere, opening the pressure safety valve, encouraged me to pause and look up.

"Please, can I help?" The young man unblocked the sink in no time and then, to my astonishment mopped the floor.

"My Knight in shining armour," I said with relief and my face reddened with embarrassment.

"In a tee-shirt, is this okay.?"

"I have not seen you in church before," I said. "Nice to welcome new members of the congregation."

"Nice to be here. Please, where is the Priest?"

"Ah, the Vicar. Reverend Wilberforce Trent," I replied. "He is in the hall, trying to play peace maker. We could have a multi coloured door - always room for compromise if we try."

The young man looked lost. "Sorry? Which door do I need to go through?"

"I apologise - don't mean to confuse you. It's just an internal squabble. All families have ups and downs. The Vicar will be busy for a while. Can I give him a message?"

"Yes, please. I am Johannes Norvik. I need to find my room."

"I am so sorry! I did not know you were arriving today. We were told to expect you in the middle of June. Oh, please excuse my manners. My name is Ruth. I am afraid you caught me on a busy day."

"Pleased to meet you, Ruth. Yes, June was the original plan. Hillary Sheppard said I can arrive today. I hope this is okay?

"Oh, did he?" I was perplexed by the arrangements but held back from asking more questions. I thought. '*don't shoot the messenger*.' "I will have a chat with him later. Most importantly, welcome to Old Botlean and St Laurence. Come and sit down in the hall. Can I get you a drink?"

***

Wilberforce stood in the middle of Mrs Redbridge and Mrs Sharpe as they charged forward in the battle of the door. They fixed bayonets (metaphorically speaking). Their words pierced through the barricades stubbornly constructed to delay the progress of the opposing preference. Wilberforce stood, exhausted and humiliated, in the inaugural 'Bring and Share Lunch' in the Church Hall. An idea put forward and managed by his wife who was mortified by the scene unravelling in front of her eyes. Hannah tried to distract the guests with the help of Molly, who was singing verses from '*Galway Bay*', and Ivee who was sharing ideas about activities for the proposed Summer Club albeit for a couple of weeks, in August.

"Ladies, please," Wilberforce's initial request was ignored so the volume raised alarmingly for all those in the hall, but it achieved the desired result. "Please. Krystal, and you, Doris. Please can we be considerate of the other guests who would like to enjoy their Sunday lunch in peace. Hannah and all the volunteers have worked incredibly hard to prepare for this joyful event and serve the church family today. We will continue this conversation in the next PCC meeting, and in Faith by that time there will be a harmonious compromise. Now, I am sure Molly will be only too happy to get you some tea and cake. Thank you."

"You tell 'em, Vicar." Logan, the caretaker, grumbled. Molly elbowed him in the ribs which delivered her message more clearly than mere words.

Johannes looked aghast at the unexpected incident in a church hall especially on a Sunday.

"Wilberforce," I said. "Excuse me. I know you have a lot on your plate, but may I introduce you to Johannes Norvik."

"Johannes, welcome." Wilberforce's attempt to be upbeat, fell flat, and who could have blamed him.

My grin was unbecoming and uncomfortable. "Johannes is the exchange student. He arrived from Oslo this morning."

"Long way to travel for a shared lunch," Humphrey Crook guffawed at his own joke. Unfortunately, no one joined in with his merriment and I was not aware one of the Church Wardens was involved in the welcome party.

"You are quite right, Humphrey," Wilberforce replied. "Would you mind getting Johannes a drink and a sandwich?"

"Delighted," Humphrey replied. "I am afraid the kitchen is absent of Friele Frokostkaffe, young man. Will instant coffee be acceptable? We do not have open faced sandwiches, but our closed smoked salmon sandwiches are scrumptious. How many would you like?"

Johannes was stunned at the level of Humphrey's knowledge and his eccentricity. He stuttered and stumbled, "thank you. All sounds nice. Please can I have a glass of water."

"Of course, young man," Humphrey's high-spirited response lowered the heat of the tension.

Wilberforce apologised to Johannes for the lack of readiness. I introduced Johannes to some unruffled members of the congregation and at the same time tried to find Hillary, the associate Vicar.

There was a fraught silence when I informed Hannah of Johannes' arrival.

"Oh my," she was almost in tears. "I am sure Hillary said 9th of June? The day after Trooping The Colour? Oh dear, what is wrong with me?"

"There is absolutely nothing wrong with you," I said assertively. "You are exhausted, and Hillary is occupied with other matters or should I say another person. When I find him, I will ask for an explanation. Leave it to me." I thought, "*I'm getting to sound like mum each day – how scary.*"

Hannah's level of anxiety skyrocketed, and she said, "what am I going to do? The annexe is being refurbished. There is no electricity or water supply. I know, I'll move the girls in together. Will be okay for a couple of weeks. Thankfully, Hillary is staying with his friend."

The colour from Hannah's face drained into the pool of despair and self-doubt pressed down on her shoulders.

I reached out to touch her arm and said, "There is no need to disrupt your daughters. It is important for them to have a safe space and privacy. I have a spare room and plenty of space. Please do not worry."

"You are so kind," Hannah exhaled. "Thank God you are here to support us. I need to ask for Wilberforce's approval for safeguarding purposes, you understand, don't you? We trust you implicitly."

***

I felt quite nervous when Johannes crossed the threshold into my home. This was the first single man sharing the delicate steps of my beloved husband. The occasional visit by workmen do not count in this context.

The Scandinavian cultural link was poignant. Peder from Denmark and Johannes from Norway. I tried not to read too much into the surreal set of circumstances and held onto the fact that God is the author of creation and of each hour and day in my life.

Johannes stood in front of the painting of Møns Klint; mesmerised by the scenery set out in fine strokes of paint. "Magnificent," he said. "Island of Møn, yes? South from Copenhagen?"

"You are right," I replied. "Well spotted."

"Thank you." Johannes looked quizzically at me. "Not sure of the word spotted?"

"Please excuse me," I replied and blushed at not considering the use of colloquialism. "Peder. My husband often reminded me to be mindful of my language. His comment was good natured and well-intended, especially when visiting his family in Denmark. Peder is the artist of the magnificent painting. He was blessed with a gift beyond any understanding. No professional training – no sitting in art classes for years and no exam marks. Purely from his heart."

"Amazing," Joahnnes said. He paused and I could see the clogs in his brain ticking as he tried to find the correct words to explore a sensitive subject. "Would be great to meet Peder but you said, was blessed? Has he left?"

"Sorry," I replied. "I really must learn, or should I say, learn again, how to give a clearer description. My husband passed away; died in 2018. In fact, last year. Very strange. Seems a long time ago but I turn a corner and it feels as if it was only yesterday." It dawned on me that my usual *talk to myself moments* was being aired in public with an audience who was looking extremely baffled.

"Forgive me," I said. "Too many words."

Johannes remained silent. The long travel arrangements and bizarre introduction to St Laurence weighed heavily on his mind. He was enthralled with the depiction of the chalk cliffs crumbling into the Baltic Sea on the island of Møn which brought back memories for him. He turned from the painting and asked an abstract question. "Do you believe in Fairy Tales?"

The content of the enquiry took me back however after the content of his day up until this point, nothing would surprise me. I replied, "yes, but they do not always have happy endings. Whereas Faith and Trust will lead to eternity. I will let Wilberforce explain further after you have had some rest. There is a Christianity Explored course soon."

"Thank you," Johannes said with a thirst for knowledge. "I very much look forward to asking questions - hopefully not too many."

I smiled and sympathised with his surreal introduction to Old Botlean and said, "it is important to learn and even more important to listen." I used to get so frustrated when trying to get Peder's attention when he was painting. He did not need earplugs he was immersed in his artistry - a gift that defined him. His dedication to each brush stroke was delightful to watch. I will always be thankful we met. When Peder found out the date of my birthday he said, "we are written in the stars." My birthday is on 23rd June - Sankt Hans Aften: in Denmark – a night to celebrate summer in the company of friends and family. Embedded in my heart is the year when Peder took me to fairytale city of Odense on Fyn (Funen) island, to see the huge traditional bonfire in the meadow of Fruens Bøge: lighting up the sky and reflecting how the Holy Spirit enlightened our lives. Odense is the birthplace of Denmark's world-famous author Hans Christian Andersen in 1805. The reference to fairytales by Johannes caused a chill to run down my spine but again forced myself not to read too much into the coincidence.

"I am so happy for you. Sorry! I mean sorry. Excuse me, I am muddled." Johannes was flustered.

"No, you are not muddled," I replied offering reassurance. "No one knows what to say or do when facing grief. How strange. Why do we feel so awkward about the one topic we will all face? There is no escape." I choked back the tears and wiped my nose. "This hay fever is terrible." I tried to hide the distress and coughed to make the symptoms more authentic. "Anyway, let's focus on brighter subjects. First, are you hungry?"

"Yes, very. Shall I go to a restaurant?"

"There is no need for a restaurant," I said with raised spirits. "My mother is cooking Sunday roast. It is very tasty and popular – tickets for seats at the table sell out fast."

"How much are the tickets?" Johannes asked and appeared worried as he searched in his wallet.

"Forgive me, I am only joking. You are more than welcome - no ticket - no charge. We need to be there at 5 o'clock. Later than usual on my mum's timetable. She knows I lose track of time when volunteering. I'll show you where your room is. You can freshen up if you wish."

"Thank you. Would be very nice." I could see the relief on Johannes' face as he welcomed the opportunity to have a respite from the chaotic couple of hours.

"I'll phone mum to let her know," I called out to the void at the top of the stairs.

I thought, '*mum has probably already received the breaking news on the gossip grapevine.*'

***

CHAPTER 11

"20 BOTTLES!!" That's it. Sure it's 20 or 18?" Hillary Sheppard's outburst rebounded against each corner in The Old Door Inn.

Ivee giggled with equal enthusiasm and then said, "Sshh! You'll give the answer away to the other teams. What is a Nebuchadnezzar?"

"We'll explain later," said Lester, the Postmaster, with an unusual hint of irritation.

Wilberforce look alarmed, not only in reaction to the loud exclamation by Hillary, but also by Ivee's persistent pursuit of him. I nodded slowly to give a signal of reassurance that the situation is under control. Wilberforce visibly sighed and sat back in his chair. However, his moment of serenity was sharply shaken as Ivee shrieked, "Oh. Oooh! Oh! I know this. I know this," in response to the next question.

Geraldine pulled my arm, "Leave this one to you. Miss Geeky of Royal Knowledge."

I started to write the answer and Johannes whispered the year "1926. My grandmother was born on same day as The Queen, I mean Queen of your country, not our Queen Margrethe. Sorry, too many words. My mother is also, royal geek – is that correct word?"

Geraldine coughed to try to stifle her cackle. "Well, your mother and Ruth have a lot in common."

Johannes blushed which made his appearance more vulnerable. "No, sorry. I do not want to be rude."

"That's alright. "Geraldine smirked. "Ruth has a thick skin."

"If you weren't my best friend, I would ask you to leave."

"No, you wouldn't." Geraldine replied with the speed of lightning.

"Alright," I acquiesced. "No, I wouldn't but I wouldn't buy you any more peanuts."

"I am so scared," Geraldine said mockingly. "You'll protect me, won't you Johannes?"

Johannes looked bemused and laughed hesitantly. "You are joking?"

"Yes," Geraldine replied reassuringly. "We have been friends for longer than your years and our jokes are even older."

The raucous atmosphere in The Old Door Inn was competitive in a friendly way. Declan and Penny are wonderful hosts and bat off the banter with ease. Declan announced the winners.

"Ladies and Gentlemen," he tapped an empty glass with a spoon. "Ladies and Gentlemen, can I have your attention. You can finish your beer and chatter in a minute. You can also start tucking into the very tasty food we have prepared." The customers laughed and looked up in anticipation.

"The votes have been counted and verified by my wife and Pat's dog, Danny: thankfully, he did not eat them. So, in no particular order. Sorry, thought I was on Strictly. In reverse order; third place it's team, '*Church Open Door*.' A big round of applause please. Come on everyone, you can do better than that, for the Vicar and his team." Wilberforce gave a thumbs up in an awkward social manoeuvre. I felt sorry for him but knew he enjoyed mixing with the community and this was a first faltering step in front of a wider audience.

"Drum roll, please," Declan called out and set the scene for his wife's participation in the nerve racking few moments (metaphorically speaking.) Penny tapped her hands on the bar.

"Louder please," said Declain. "We need to build up the tension." He laughed in unison with his wife. Sharing a sense of relief and rejoicing because the first quiz night involving the new Vicar, was well attended and a success.

"Ladies and gentlemen, there is a draw between team '*Sun Flowers*' and team '*Remember the Good Old Days.*' Quiet please. As set out in the rules and regulations, which I have just made up – the two team captains to come forward to answer the tie breaker. So, Ruth and John, please take centre stage."

I gasped. "I cannot answer a question in front of everyone. Geraldine, you go!"

"Slight problem, "Geraldine replied with a mischievous twinkle in her eye. "I'm not the team captain and we don't look alike; thank goodness."

"Stop it." I snapped. "Do something!"

Geraldine stood up and said, "Excuse me, can we send a substitute please? Our team captain has an injury – she has just come down with 'scaredy cat syndrome."

The whole pub roared with laughter.

I pinched Geraldine's arm. "Ow!" she screeched. "You told me to do something."

"Not humiliate me," I retorted.

"Please let me help," Johannes said with a genuine willingness to ease the pain. "I will go, if okay?"

I looked at the other members of our team – Scarlet, a Church Warden, and Kiyana, head of the junior choir, and Joshua Jaffa, a student working in Winchester. They all nodded in agreement.

"Come on up you two," Declan's jovial invitation continued with introductions. So, we have John and John – is that the correct pronunciation?"

The response was offered sheepishly, "It is Johannes."

"Sorry young man. Did you say Johnny?"

"That is okay. Please, I do not want to stop you." Johannes looked ill at ease. He turned to me, and I returned his search for acceptance with a soft smile.

"Are you ready?" Declan asked. "Ladies and gentlemen. Silence please! I can only accept the first answer. I need to be able to hear the response clearly."

The tension built in The Old Door Inn. The atmosphere turned from jovial to a joust.

***

Peder enjoyed quizzes but did not really enjoy pubs. We went to one quiz organised by the previous social committee in the Church Hall: not all members of the congregation approved or, should I say, accepted Peder. May have been a mistrust of a foreigner of an expectation I would marry someone my own age with a professional career. Dad tried to be a Quiz Master on Christmas Day in 2017, my last Christmas with my darling husband who was my world. Dad's home-made quiz did not go to plan. It was devoid of accurate answers. We resorted to the boardgame Trivial Pursuit and Dad won the Boxing Day chess tournament.

***

Oyez, (pronounced 'oh yay') oyez, oyez!" Declan's impersonation of a Town Crier resulted in most of the guests expressing puzzlement and the rattling of his keys instead of a large hand bell gave rise to a ripple of laughter.

"Just get on with it!" Pat protested. "I want a Guinness before closing time."

Declan cleared his throat and then asked. "Copenhagen is the capital of which country?"

"DENMARK!" Johannes shouted.

"Well done, young man. That's the correct answer. Here is your trophy and I'll bring over the bottle of champagne in a minute. So, Sunflowers are the winners of Quiz Night - June 10."

"Congratulations," Joshua said and patted the victor on his back. "You kept cool. You won."

"No. We won." Johannes looked at me and smiled. "Sun Flowers are top of the chart?"

Geraldine pulled my arm and said, "come on, we'll get the champagne and glasses. Declan is busy."

"Please, I can help?" Johannes asked eagerly.

"No!" Geraldine replied forcefully. "Sorry, thank you for offering. We are fine. Joshua wants to tell you all about his work in the graduate scheme in the Property Services Team of Hampshire County Council. Sounds fascinating."

"You are using him." Geraldine's observation hit home.

"No," I replied defensively. "Just helping him."

"You are helping yourself!" Geraldine's tough love can be extremely tough when required. "He reminds you of Peder and you are just trying to cling on to keep the memory alive. Help him – yes, but do not become emotionally involved. Johannes will be leaving soon, and you cannot keep him locked in your house. I mean, Johannes will not stay here because of you. Age gaps of 34 years can work, but it is usually when the men are older."

I get so annoyed when Geraldine is right which is most of the time. She could see the reality reluctantly sinking in and gave me a hug.

"Congratulations," dad said loudly with a sense of pride mixed with a perception that I needed reassurance. "I knew there's a brain in there somewhere."

"Love you too, dad," I replied. "I inherited the one brain cell from you. Thankfully not your looks."

"Ouch! Below the belt." Dad's comical comment calmed down with a concern; disguised as an observation. "Johannes is an intelligent your man. Understand he is moving in with the Vicar soon. I am glad Steven's son, Joshua, could make it. He's really bright, and great Johannes can go to the New Forest activity week with him. All for the best. Yes?"

I looked directly at dad and knew he had my best interest at the forefront of his mind when he invited the son of a member of the golf club. Mum and dad know my heart is shattered and will not mend by using plasters or substitutes.

***

CHAPTER 12

The deep clean of the church and hall usually takes place every three months dependant on the number of volunteers available. The kitchen would take three months to clean if every nook and cranny were investigated. Thankfully, the rota showed my name in the church hall duty team on the June schedule. The tasks include cleaning the cupboards and washing the tables with anti-bacterial spray. Mopping the floor is the last duty of the day. Surprisingly rewarding to smell the freshness and see a shiny floor. Alas, the scene is a brief encounter before the activity of church family life re-emerges with gusto.

I was convinced the holes, in my baggy, bubble gum pink, tee -shirt with dazzling gold glittery letters on the front, spelling 'LOVE ME' would not raise an eyebrow. The other volunteers would be far too busy to notice the oversized paint splattered casual trousers. Peder kept them specifically for the 'deep clean' duties. The cord from Peder's dressing gown made a tremendous belt for my waist. My trainers were on my feet and not in my wardrobe – a good start to what promised to be a fruitful day.

The rustling and chatter from the church hall filled me with reassurance. I thought, '*Wilberforce's recruiting campaign is gathering momentum.*'

I tripped up the loose step, dropped my rucksack and shouted, "BOOP!"

The reaction was far different than anticipated. "SURPRISE!" The guests of my unexpected and dare I say unwelcome birthday afternoon tea called out and assumed I would rejoice in their greeting. In retrospect my response was selfish and unbecoming in a church hall.

"Oh. Right! Do you know it's deep clean day?"

"All done," said Hannah with glee. "No need to worry. You can get changed. The Ladies toilet has been spruced up specially for you."

I scowled at Geraldine and mouthed, "changed?"

Geraldine scuttled over and said, "SURPRISE!"

"Alright. We've done all the that," I retorted. "What am I going to change into?"

Geraldine replied scathingly, "I don't know? Change into a Fairy or more appropriately change into someone with manners. At least try and look grateful."

"Sorry." I replied remorsefully with reddened facial features. "Just a little embarrassing with everyone wearing pretty summer dresses and I'm in the pretty awful Mrs Mop outfit."

"I totally agree with you, which doesn't happen very often," Geraldine giggled and continued, "Basil's outfit is not quite pretty, and John is wearing his best grey trousers." Geraldine's humour helped me to relax.

Dad bellowed out his greeting, "how's my favourite daughter?" He hugged me knowing it would add to the embarrassment.

"I am your only daughter, unless you need to tell us something?"

"Not at all." The dad jokes continued relentlessly. "You could have made an effort. I'm sure your mother has a spare dress at the back of her numerous wardrobes."

Geraldine laughed loudly.

"Dad, will you stop, please!" My request was delivered with exasperation. I turned to Geraldine, "please stop laughing, you're only encouraging him."

I saw mum walking towards me with disdain written all over her face. "Blodwyn, do you have any other clothes with you? Hannah might have a spare dress?"

"Thank you, mum," I replied with my lips pursed. "If I knew there was an afternoon tea, my fashion choice would have been different. As it is a surprise, I am afraid this will have to do. By the time I get home, iron a dress and return, Logan would have locked up. And how do you think I can possibly get into one of Hannah's dresses? They are far too small."

Mum took the outburst with remarkably good spirit and said, "Blodwyn, come have a Chamomile tea, calm yourself down."

Geraldine whispered to mum, "hormones."

"I heard that!" I snapped.

***

Johannes presented the sunflowers and an iconic blue tin of Royal Dansk Danish butter cookies, with gracious charm and sensitivity. His body language and choice of words depicted a soul far more mature than his outward appearance.

"Thank you." I blushed.

"I like your tee shirt," Johannes gave the compliment politely.

"Yes," I replied. "It's in the autumn/winter collection of all the top fashion houses. This is a special viewing of the new label - Trendy at Fifty."

"More like, Frumpy at Fifty," said Geraldine.

"Please excuse me, I leave now." Johannes said with a tinge of sadness.

"Blimey, our jokes must be getting worse. Hope we have not scared you too much?" Geraldine enquired.

"No. You look very funny. Sorry, your jokes are very funny. I am muddled. Joshua is playing tennis, and I am going." Johannes stuttered and seemed reluctant to leave, but we both knew the departure was the wisest strategic move. He leant over and kissed my cheek. I wiped the tear gliding down my cheek and mumbled, "this hay fever is getting worse."

***

"Aunty, what a funny outfit."

"All the better to take selfies with!" I said to my twelve-year-old niece who looked horrified at my appearance. The arrival of my brother, Gareth, and his wife, Beatrice, and my nephew and niece was an added bonus to the afternoon full of surprises.

Gareth gave me a formal kiss on the cheek and Beatrice conducted the protocol of three kisses. I respect the Swiss custom however find it incredibly embarrassing: I turn my head when I not supposed to and knock noses. Beatrice is empathetic to my clumsy effort.

"How is my younger sister?" Gareth asked. His accent sounds more Swiss each time we meet which is sadly not often.

"Not so young," Geraldine piped up and smiled at my brother.

"Nice gold glitter top," Beatrice's attempt at a compliment was strained.

"Different style than normal?" said Gareth before instructing his son to give me a present. "Come on Cedwyn, give Aunty Ruth her present. You and Ursula spent a long time wrapping and writing cards."

"Happy birthday, Aunty." Cedwyn's tentative greeting was followed by an earnest request to protect his '*street cred*' or should I say his reputation. "Please can we make photos later?"

"Yes, of course. I fully understand – this outfit will not get many likes on Facebook?"

"You'll probably get banned," Geraldine's joke went down well with her young audience, and she lapped up the applause (metaphorically speaking.)

"We look forward to your birthday dinner," said Beatrice.

"Which time is the booking?" Gareth asked.

"Please ask the boss," I said, and he acknowledged my words knowingly.

Mum had booked a table at Tylney Hall: the same venue as my wedding reception. A far larger table than I had anticipated bearing in mind the extra guests.

The choice of venue was not a cruel decision but an incentive to reconcile my grief. Inside the birthday card from mum and dad the greeting included the words: 'Love the memories and love today with hope for tomorrow."

***

"No balloons then?" Geraldine asked me. "Bit mean, don't you think?"

"Balloons are banned," I replied. "Don't think Hannah will allow them anywhere near the Church again after what happened at Easter."

I looked at the setting of colourful tea pots and matching cups and cake stands and said, "remember the days when we went out for a drink? Now it has declined to Afternoon Tea. Don't get me wrong, it is nice and will not have to get a taxi home!"

"Or recover from a hangover," Geraldine quipped.

"We weren't that bad?"

"Only when the Babycham came out," Geraldine replied, "hit you between your eyes and still hurt the next day."

"We spent most of the time dancing." I said smiling at the memories popping into my mind.

"That's one name for it." Geraldine chuckled.

***

The stinging steps of the stilettos drew our attention to the stylish figure wearing a slim fit, button front, midi dress in burnt orange. The accessories of vibrant yellow shoes and handbag stood out amidst the sedate tea dresses and my abstract tee-shirt.

"Need our sunglasses in the glaring light," Geraldine quipped.

"Will you stop," I replied and nudged her ribs before sharing my observation. "Thought he packed his bags a long time ago?"

"Looks as if he is looking for left luggage," Geraldine replied sarcastically.

"She really is a glutton for punishment, but she won't listen to us because she thinks we are jealous or interfering old women?" I said whilst trying to discreetly look over to Bernadette and her plus one, George Andover.

"You're right with the second point. I definitely don't envy being picked up and thrown down, again and again. Love Seamus too much but don't tell him - he'll think he does not have to make an effort. Got to keep him on his toes!"

"Don't be silly you're like a pair of old slippers," I said.

"Cheers! Remind me to return the compliment."

I flustered and stuttered, "no! Mean you look comfortable together and know you won't fit with anyone else."

Hannah noticed my hand gesture and asked, "are you okay?"

"Yes, thank you. Everything is great and you've worked so hard as usual. Just wanted to ask if you could have a conversation with Bernadette?"

"You can start by asking her to introduce you to George." Geraldine interjected with a strike right to the heart of the matter.

"George?" Hannah asked.

I struggled to find the most appropriate words in the circumstances, "I am afraid Bernadette's partner, sorry, the guest she is with now – is the man she had the liaison with."

"Stop trying to be so diplomatic," Geraldine protested. "To cut a long story short: Bernadette had an affair with George who is a Hedge Fund Manager in the City of London. He is charming, rich, and married."

"Oh." Hannah was stumped for a reply after Geraldine's blunt bombardment and asked, "you mentioned someone; is this the same man?"

I glared at my life-long friend who is infuriating at times: no doubt the feeling is mutual. I smiled awkwardly at Hannah and replied, "Yes. Maybe best not to antagonise Bernadette this afternoon. Why don't I ask her to lunch, and you can, coincidently, be there?"

Before Hannah had a chance to open her lips, Geraldine jumped into the fold. "Food poisoning and lying. Not really a good example of true Christian behaviour, is it?"

"Please excuse my dearest and annoying friend," I said. "Too many chocolate fingers go to her head."

"You two are created to be in partnership," Hannah laughed.

"Like Laurel and Hardy?" Geraldine chortled.

I trod on Geraldine's foot and thought, '*that will keep her quiet for a minute whilst she sits down and rubs her minor injury.*'

Hannah smiled, unknowing of the red lump on Geraldine's toe, and said, "it is a full-time job being a Vicar's wife - loving it but am stretched in all different directions."

"A Christian family endures highs and lows like any other family." Geraldine said. "But you've got an excellent counsellor and you do not have to take out a mortgage to pay all the cost."

I was startled. "My, you have been listening!"

"Surprised myself!" Geraldine laughed.

"Quick, get her signed up to the Christianity Explored course," I said enthusiastically.

"We could ask Seamus?" Hannah asked naively.

I shook my head, and gently replied, "Seamus is very busy. He may come another time." Moving the conversation into a different direction, I thanked Hannah for all the time spent decorating the hall and lovely cakes.

"Vicky delivered them this morning at 7 o'clock. She looked worn out," said Hannah. "Wilberforce is in contact with social services, and I am trying to find out how to obtain a care plan. She'll have to sell the bakery: it'll break her heart. We have contacted her family, but they are not interested. I should not be judgemental and am sure they are busy."

Geraldine jumped in with force, "they will not be too busy when the Will is read out!"

"How sad," said Hannah as she wiped a tear from the corner of her eye.

"There are so many changes," I said mournfully. "The village will be unrecognisable soon."

"A property developer will be knocking at the door before the bakery closes," said Geraldine. "They would love to get their hands on church buildings to grab a massive prophet. Make sure to keep the doors locked at St Laurence!"

Hannah replied swiftly, "it is important to keep the doors open, and offer a warm welcome and invitation to join us."

Wilberforce walked towards us with an offer of fresh tea.

Geraldine shared her concern, "just saying you'll have to keep a tight hold of the church - developers are hoovering up land."

"If they take the building by some legal loophole, we can meet on the village green," he replied.

"But not on the same day as the cricket; those red balls can quite literally knock you for six." My attempt at a joke fell flat.

Wilberforce coughed awkwardly and continued, "at the end of the day, the bricks and mortar are just a rain shelter. It is important to meet, but the Christian family are resourceful and creative."

"You can use Ruth's house," Geraldine mischievously offered an alternative option. "It's got enough room and there is the garden for open air services."

I glared at Geraldine - she could always push my buttons.

Wilberforce intervened with the diplomacy of an ambassador and sensitivity of a father. "We will not impose on Ruth. But on the other hand, we could hold a bible study there? Might be a squash but close fellowship is beneficial."

Hannah touched her husband's arm gently. "The tea's cold now. I'll make a fresh pot. Oh yes, before I forget, Rachael would like to talk to you about the baptism."

Wilberforce looked puzzled.

Hannah shared the information with the patience of a devoted wife committed to their lifetime vocation, "Rachael and Shaun Reardon."

He scratched his head. Hannah expanded the description "The twins?" Wilberforce's face lit up with recognition. "Yes, sorry. I remember. Such a blessing to have two new strong soldiers joining the fight for Faith."

**

CHAPTER 13

"How many nights are we staying exactly?"

"Three," I replied defensively.

"So why are you packing a travel trunk?"

"Don't exaggerate," I said. "It doesn't suit you. On the other hand?" "I am bringing my *just in case* supplies," I explained. "Be prepared – motto of Girl Guides?"

"We weren't in the Girl Guides," said Geraldine with an escalation of impatience in her voice.

"Never too late!" I teased my trusted friend as the steam of exasperation started emanating from her mouth.

"You've got to do better than that, to throw me off the scent. Okay let's try another approach – where is your cabin suitcase?" Geraldine asked.

"You mean the red one with spinning wheels?" I cross questioned Geraldine sensing the boundary line was a hair's breadth away.

"You've only got one cabin suitcase?" Geraldine protested. "Unless you have a secret stash in the attic."

"No," I replied, "my supply of rucksacks are in the attic. My suitcases are at mum's."

"Give me strength, "Geraldine put her hands up to her head and took a deep breath. "Okay, I'll go to your mum's and get your small case. As a compromise, you can bring one rucksack just as a comfort blanket, so to speak."

"You are so kind," I said with a petulant shake of my head. "I'll call mum she won't mind driving over and she can bring some cakes."

"Your mum will faint if she sees this mess and will start hoovering, dusting, and ironing. Mind you she could cook us lunch?" Geraldine's cheeky grin was followed by an explanation. "Only joking. She'll be worn out, running after the grandchildren."

"And spoiling Gareth," I reacted speedily.

"Ooh! The green eye monster has escaped. See sibling rivalry is hanging on?"

"Only joking," I tried to cover up my inner prickly characteristic which is entirely unfair because mum and dad spoil me rotten. Well dad does; mum is more selective with her treats.

"No, you're not!" Geraldine retorted. "You're just jealous because Gareth, Beatrice, Cedwyn and Ursula are enjoying home cooked meals and you're on toast rations."

The front door shut forcefully as the wind of change hit the framework. I was under strict instructions to downsize the selection of clothes and shoes. I am of the belief that sitting on a case, to get it to shut, is not good for the frame. Surely, it is far better to have some space to ease the pressure on the lock. Although this logic does not work when using a supermarket trolley – more space - more special offers spilling over the sides of the metal frame.

Dad fitted the new sturdy loft ladder in January. The handle is much appreciated and needed. Navigating the steps from the loft door is precarious – dad does not like me to do this on my own however this day is different. My quest to find a suitable rucksack was diverted by the presence of my most precious memory box. Items belonging to Peder are shared and cared for in each room of my home, including the 'little room'. His framed cartoons depicting humorous scenes at the seaside are presented in pride of place. Not crude or lurid but reflecting his interpretation of a traditional British culture. Dad likes them; the jury is still out with regards mum. I think she secretly hoped they would be in the archives by now, but it is not time yet and maybe it will never be.

I reached into the handcrafted wooden treasure chest which Peder designed and constructed. Our initials are engraved on the lid: the letters intertwined with swirls and curls depicting a scene of calligraphy. A small antique satin-wood money box takes on the role of a key box with aplomb and is camouflaged in the sheep's wool loft insulation. The solitary key clings to a sterling silver bracelet accompanied by a St Christopher pendant. The matching small segment of shaped metal; the key to our harmonious song, was cradled in the hands of my dearest, cherished and treasured husband as he laid peacefully in the white willow coffin. Sunflowers framed the sunset of a free spirit. His favourite navy-blue scarf with paisley patterns on a deep-red background, complemented by orange accents, settled under the wedding day attire – a light blue tweed, vintage, three-piece, tailored fit, single-breasted suit, bedecked with two buttons designed and sewn on by the bridegroom. Far too casual for mum's standards but quite literally suited Peder's character.

A reinforced cardboard removal box contained the supply of rucksacks we shared. The frayed pockets of the one I carried when our two worlds collided in the art gallery, was next to Peder's favourite well-worn travel bag: adorned with ribbons and badges from Florence – the location of an apartment he rented after venturing from Denmark for the first time. He demonstratively portrayed descriptions of the spectacular sculptures and architecture, and art galleries with the enthusiasm of a child but with the experience of an artistic soul who found his calling and freedom to unveil his unique style. He skipped over the insight of a friendship with an older Italian artist, and I did not dwell in the past because those were his days, and I did not need to intrude into his privacy. In a moment of frivolity and a respectful fact-finding exercise to determine if an individual from the past will be knocking at the door. "Forewarned is to be forearmed" we joked but knew deep down we did not want to face an ex-wife nor husband nor children without having the information required to deal with a potentially awkward conversation. We reassured each other there were no ties to the past. All matters were settled and that was the end of the discussion. Thank God, our time together was not shredded by sinking in the quagmire of reliving past relationships. How tragic for those caught in the revolving door of regret and relentless torment of past mistakes.

I selected a rucksack Peder bought me during our last trip to Denmark: it held sentimental value with a manageable level of emotional encirclement. Peder would not go to a 'manufactured spa' as he called them but would have never stopped me taking mum for a treat. Dad relished the day off and Peder lost himself in his painting. Peder was comfortable in his own skin. He did not need to put obstacles on the path to my interests or '*lady days*'. Recollections from our time apart were shared in a relaxed story telling style. His panache with a paint brush was equalled by his mesmerising style of writing fictional tales and poetry. The rejections from publishers did not deter his determination. Sadly, he ran out of time to see the fulfilment of his dream - a novel on the shelves of a bookstore, but the drafts are stored safely in the walnut and leaded glass bookcase, manufactured in Italy: an unusual method of payment for a painting, however we embraced the vintage, mid-century style.

***

"Have you fallen asleep up there?" Geraldine called out.

"No. Be down in a minute," I replied. I locked the memory box and returned the key tenderly into our shelter.

"Do you want any help?" Geraldine asked before delivering a line with her wicked sense of humour. "Surprised you can still fit through the loft door after your birthday meal and cake."

"Did dad tell you to say that? Sounds like one of his jokes. Just catch this will you?" I threw the bag which unintentionally landed on Geraldine's head.

"There's no need to be vicious," she complained.

We reconvened in the living room. Piles of my clothes on the settee, the empty large suitcase in the hall and the tiny, in my view, cabin bag balanced on the foot stall. We tugged and pulled at clothes; disagreeing if they fell into the necessary, or unnecessary or just ridiculous category.

"We have to bring slippers, it's on the website. At least one of us has carried out some research." I boasted.

"Listen to miss smarty pants or should I say miss big pants. Yes, bring our slippers, but that doesn't mean thermal slipper socks with a cute knit ribbon on the top."

"It might be cold," I smiled. "They're my favourite."

"Favourite for Christmas not for the middle of June," Geraldine said with a tormented look her face. "You must have slippers from the spa day with your mum – you don't throw anything away."

"Why are you so grumpy?" I asked. "You are already suited and booted. Living room looks like a jumble sale."

I admire how Geraldine manages three children and her husband who is totally reliant on her house managerial skills. Goodness knows the extent of chaos which would befall her home if she had to go away for more than a week. Seamus knows my mum would step into the breech because he does not have any family support which is incredibly sad, but he accepts the circumstances with a stoicism strengthened by the strong roots of a steadfast marriage.

"Will do us good to have time to chat and reflect." My comment surprised me as much as Geraldine.

"Don't get all spiritual on me - we have to concentrate on packing your clothes."

"I'm wearing a bikini at all times," I said. "Okay, big pants bikini - never got the hang of thongs - excuse the pun!"

"Who are you kidding?" Geraldine refuted my packing plan. "Where's your swimming costume and floral swimming cap?"

"I can't wear a swimming costume when having a massage," my enquiry was met with a sharp reply and Geraldine did not miss the open goal. "What type of massage have you booked? It's just your shoulders not down there which I'm sure is not tidy?"

"How rude!" I tried to look offended but could not stifle my laughter.

As a compromise, I selected shorts and large vest tops with room to manoeuvre.

The packing debacle lasted longer than anticipated. Geraldine took bread from the freezer to make toast and cheese sandwiches. I squashed another few extra pair of pants into the corners of my luggage – '*just in case*.'

"Your mum gave me a tin of fairy cakes, they smell gorgeous," Geraldine hummed as she absorbed the aroma of freshly baked delights.

There was no milk in the fridge therefore we settled on peppermint tea as an accompaniment to our ad-hoc lunch.

My rucksack toppled onto the floor as I forced more cereal bars into every gap.

"What are they?" Geraldine looked at the draft invitations to the Summer Club.

"Ivee asked me to look at her designs and proofread the content, it won't take long," I explained tentatively.

"NO! ABSOLUTELY, NO" Geraldine's frustration catapulted her voice up to the kitchen ceiling. "You are having a break from volunteering. Helping the church is laudable but the strain is weighing you down. Let others take up the slack. I am sure Hillary will be only too delighted to overlook her work. If he is too busy trying to impress the vicar, there are many others more than able to read a piece of paper."

"Don't be so mean," I replied. "Ivee is on the receiving end of so much criticism: this may help to boost her confidence. I'll call her to arrange a time next week – she loves going for a hot chocolate."

"I am not being rude," Geraldine's disagreement with my suggestion sprung into sight. "Well, actually, I'm being very rude but truthful: she can make a cup of hot chocolate and arrange a time with someone else. Doris will tell Ivee, sorry, mean help. Will give her something else to think about other than the colour of the church door."

"You can be truly ruthless at times," I retorted but knew she was right. "We could really do with your direct discipline during the Summer Club activities in the Church Hall."

"No thanks. I've got enough to manage at home - might help for a few hours, if you're lucky, and only if you reduce the number of hours volunteering. Deal?"

"Okay, you win again," I groaned before asking. "Bring the boys and Siobhán– will be good fun."

"No, they don't want to go to summer activities - unless they can go in disguise." Geraldine's reply seemed scathing, however reflected the wisdom of a mother who instinctively knows, the fallout from forcing her children to go, would far exceed the fun factor.

"They can help with younger ones?" I suggested.

"Not a good idea – they're not bad; drive me to distraction at times but compared to others they are angels." Geraldine continued. "I've booked a couple of weeks in Scotland. Can't face the crowds and delays at airports so we're travelling on an overnight train to Edinburgh - that should be fun. I am praying there is some sort of connection to Wi-Fi, or we'll have a riot on our hands. There is a major drama, as they call it, if they're away from their mobiles for ten minutes."

"Slightly exaggerating?" I smirked.

"Yes, alright," Geraldine conceded. "Seamus is worse than them. His laptop is banned: your mum is going to keep it under lock and key."

"Will be a lovely break for you and an exciting adventure for the children."

"Kids think we will be on the Flying Scotsman. I won't burst their bubble just yet, but no doubt Seamus will cave into their questioning during the next few days. Siobhán twists him around her little finger. Never mind, we'll make it up to them. A selfie with the Loch Ness monster should do the trick. Seamus already has the costume."

"Honestly, you are more childish than the children, at times," I laughed. "Why don't you hire a car like they did in the James Bond film - travel around the stunning scenery. What was the name of the film? Goldfinger?"

"Nearly," Geraldine sniggered. "Only about fifty years difference. It is Skyfall. And before you ask, we are not hiring an Aston Martin, and Seamus cannot fit into a tight suit even though he has been on a slim soup diet."

I tipped my head and asked, "how did they make that journey without having a natural break? Even worse, without a bottle of water and cereal bars?"

"So, you think they should have had a flask and picnic basket?" Geraldine quipped.

"Could've claimed it on expenses?" I giggled.

Geraldine huffed and puffed. "You're being even more ridiculous than you normally are. Anyway, back to the real world, and that bulging rucksack?

"I'll just take a few more breakfast bars."

"They do have a restaurant in the hotel; your mum and dad have paid for full board, so we won't go hungry. We are not going on a detox diet or lettuce leaf diet like Miss Fickle - Stick."

"Who?" I could not think of the answer to the cryptic clue.

"Keep up," Geraldine tutted. "Miss Angie, my case is under the bed; packed and ready to go, Teacher."

"Stop it!" I shrieked. "Your nails are sharper than mum's talons."

"Now you are being really silly," Geraldine replied. "Your mum is Queen of Claws."

"I'll bring the rejects upstairs," Geraldine mumbled from under the bundle of clothes from the ridiculous category.

"Mind the hoover and ironing board at the top of the stairs," I called out earnestly, but was too late – she tripped over the hoover brush head and expressed an expletive followed by an apology.

"You need to get a storage cupboard downstairs or under the stairs, if you ever get around to clearing all the rubbish out."

"What rubbish?" I protested. Geraldine threw the dishevelled pile of clothes on the bed in the spare room.

"I'll ask dad," I said. "He can build a few storage cupboards but the guttering and roof need fixing first."

"I know your dad is still active and annoying," Geraldine replied, "but you can't expect him to climb up on the roof. And even if one of Declan's friends does the work, it's still going to cost a fortune. I don't think you've got enough money in your piggy bank."

"Sore subject," I pouted. "My pretty piggy bank broke and mum made me use a red Elastoplast tin."

"You mean, just like the one under the stairs?" Geraldine's radar picks up every inch of my belongings except those in the loft which she knows are there, but also knows the sensitivity surrounding them.

Her expression straightened and I sensed the sombre comment waiting on her lips. "Seriously though, it would help to have a smaller place?"

"Exactly how small?" I asked abruptly.

"Less space means less clutter. We think it may help with dealing with the grief."

"Good to hear you've had a meeting without me," I snapped. "Where did you have it – in the Church Hall?"

"No, silly. We're all worried about you and how your home is increasingly becoming a shrine to Peder." Geraldine gulped and realised the choice of words, on this occasion, were insensitive and inappropriate. The content of her comment seared through my heart. Of course, she was right but too soon, far too soon, to remove displays of Peder's photos, artistry, and accomplishments.

I have heard someone say, '*after death, pictures of us go from, prominence of display in the home, to the back of the shelf, into the drawer, into storage boxes, and finally into recycling.*' Tremendously sad; however, there is an ounce of truth within the observation. My thoughts are, '*we go from being talked about each week, then just on birthdays, anniversaries, and Christmas. However, the gaps in time lengthen, and within a few short years many do not remember our place in the family tree nor our favourite food, films, or fables.*'

Geraldine hugged me and said, "I'm really sorry. We both need some R&R. I need to give my mouth a rest, and you need to relax - make sure to pack your earplugs."

I raised my head and tried to lighten the tension. "Anyway, I cannot downsize, what about the Bible study and fellowship groups? They need the space?"

"Yes, St Laurence needs you," Geraldine replied. "But not 24/7. Anyway, Humphrey has a mansion. Might be filled with eccentric items like him but they could fit an army in there."

"Not sure his detached house is a mansion, but it will need a super spring clean if the gossip girls are right. Sorry, I should not listen to the tittle tattle," I laughed and continued. "I do not like change., want to settle in one place now."

"Don't give up," Geraldine sparkled with encouragement and cheekiness. "The only constant is change. Make the most of each day. Who knows what tomorrow brings?"

"Always liked Richard Gere," I said. "How many times have we watched Officer and a Gentleman?"

"Lost count," Geraldine replied. "If anyone tried to pick you up, they would end up in hospital."

"Hah! Hah! Very funny," I pretended to laugh. "But, I must give up chocolate."

"Really!?!" Geraldine shrieked. "You will need to find an iron will or an iron padlock for your chocolate tin. Before you ask, yes, I know where you hide the tin."

"Okay, Mrs Shirley Holmes, gloat why don't you – solved another mystery."

Geraldine ushered me into the living room encouraging me to sit on my case for the final time and fix the padlock which I am sure is not entirely necessary when travelling by train to Brockenhurst but provides reassurance and an illusion of travelling by aeroplane with Peder.

"After our revitalising weekend, we will be bright eyed and bushy tailed, and can chat about all the adventures you can have. A new you, a new start." Geraldine pronounced the plans for the future which sounded so easy when said quickly.

"A new start? Doing what?"

"Write a book, sing a song, climb every mountain!" Geraldine giggled at her own jokes which I did not think were amusing – just filled my crowded mind with more options. "On second thoughts, don't climb a mountain – you'll need the emergency services and don't sing a song, because we'll need the emergency services to treat the damage to our ears. So that leaves, writing a book; you've got time on your hands and wanted to be an author since primary school. But make sure it is not a biography – it'll be sooo boring!"

"Cheers," I replied. "Turn over a new leaf – start a new chapter."

Geraldine put her hands over her ears and said, "That's enough. If we come out with any more clichés, we'll fade into the background."

I made one more cup of tea before we left; a chance to raid the chocolate tin and to check the content of my rucksack, for the third time. Mum's check out list is infuriating, at times, and dad is the referee of the conflict of priorities, however I miss her when packing to go away – an enjoyable experience with Peder however I have lost the enthusiasm and courage to travel far. At times, activity close to home hits me harder with the sense of loss. Initially, I could hardly get to the check out at the supermarket without blubbing – crying. Not that Peder was a great grocery shopper but willingly pushed a heavy trolley and carried the bags to his green 1960s Morris Minor 1000 Traveller, which I sold shortly after his death. Somethings were too painful to keep – facing the car outside our home tore another strip off my resilience which I could not sew back on. Declan found a buyer – one of the regulars at The Old Door Inn, generously paid over the market price, and moved it away quickly. I kept the vintage woollen striped travel blanket which is cosy in the loft.

"When you get your travel legs back on, you can go to Zürich spend time with Gareth and Beatrice. Cedwyn and Ursula will be only too delighted to introduce you to their friends so you can embarrass them with your crazy clothes."

"Gareth works until silly o'clock," I replied with a tinge of regret rooted in not spending much time with my brother. "Will be nice to rest by the lake with Beatrice and go on the boat trip with the kids as long as I remember a sick bag after the last time."

"Think the children are still traumatised and all the other passengers," Geraldine chortled. "Keep your feet on dry land and enjoy Swiss Chocolate, Rösti, and the pièce de résistance – go to Sprüngli - best sandwiches and cakes – ever! Beside your mum's cakes, of course!"

"I'd like to go to Austria," I said as the hope of travelling came into the line of sight.

"There's an idea," Geraldine said excitedly. She stood up to re-enact the iconic scene and called out, "run over the hill and sing." She stopped in her tracks. "On second thoughts, skip that idea. Go to Odense; visit the Hans Christian Anderson house museum for inspiration. You went with Peder, didn't you?"

"Yes," I uttered with melancholy attached to each word, "but it won't be the same."

"No, sadly nothing is going to be the same; different, but never the same. We need to find new adventures, and we will. We better start soon old girl, otherwise we'll run out of time."

"You are so ageist, "I retorted. "Do you think we can shake off the past?"

"Yes, I think so; for the precious positive past we don't want to remove it, so we wear it in a different way. We will never throw it away – we learn to live with it and for the most part it is a comforting companion as long as it does not control our every move. For the poisonous past relationships – we need to admit they happened, to ourselves, I don't mean make a national broadcast."

"I know," I confessed. "Did enough of that in London. The worst lies are the ones we tell ourselves, and bizarrely think, no one will know!"

"You and me both," said Geraldine, "although, I think Bernadette wins first prize in that category."

"We were all as bad as each other." My reply took Geraldine by surprise because it was served with the same sharp sauce usually dished up to me. "I can't judge her when I acted in the same way."

"You are absolutely right," Geraldine conceded and blushed which was completely out of character. I did not pry as to why, but she shared one more nugget of information, "as long as we do not try to tread water then swim back to shore, carrying the false hope, we can build a bigger sandcastle using the same grains of sand."

I thought it best to leave well alone. Her and Seamus have no strings tripping them up, so put this down to an unfortunate liaison in London when I was working at a conference.

Geraldine had not finished offering advice about the past and steered the wheel towards the brief encounters. "You've put Johannes into the safe, secure section of your mind? Yes?

I took a deep breath, nodded, and knew she was right. The tough love is needed no matter how much I want to put my hands over my ears and say, "la la la I can't hear you."

The insightful choice of Geraldines' words reflected the grief brutally sprung upon her at the tender age of twenty-one: her parents were in a fatal car accident when travelling back from a weekend in Milford-on-Sea. Geraldine declined the invitation to join them - tempted by the charming cottage, however the bright lights of London beckoned and blighted her life: survivors guilt seeped in slowly. Mum and Dad opened their arms and home to an only child who had lost her anchor. Our extended family includes Geraldine and Seamus and their children; they share the happy, surprising, and sad elements of our relationships. Geraldine's aunts and uncles drifted from shore as did her cousins. Unfortunately, Seamus' mother magnified the loss in Geraldine's life by declaring it a bad sign, even went as far as saying it was a curse, which fed into the poisonous pursuit for their relationship to fail. Dad did his duty by walking Geraldine down the aisle and made a speech at the reception with predictable dad jokes interspaced with poignant memories. Seamus took the reins and revelled in the comical narrative as did all the guests.

Geraldine is spikey; her sharp edges are steeped in waves of levity and gravity. I am blessed to have an honorary sister who encourages, and irritates, and loves me: not with soft sentiment but with a strong protective nature.

***

"Yes, I enjoyed travelling then but now, I feel safe in Old Botlean."

Geraldine tolerated my delayed reaction and replied, "good to hear. Sometimes you need to step out of your nest to rest. We'll keep chugging along and, God willing, we'll be here when you return.

Don't forget to send a postcard: like the old days. You remember? Photos of sunsets and our spelling mistakes squeezed into the small space."

***